Grabill Missionary Church Library

3 3678

W9-CBI-723

"I just hope you don't mind spending so much time with me, Rainy. This ship is full of people and I don't think you've had the opportunity to mingle with the other passengers."

I can't believe he seems to be on the verge of apologizing for spending time with me. What if he wants to be rid of me for the rest of the cruise so that he can meet other women?

"Look, Winston, if you're having second thoughts about spending the day together in Cozumel—"

"No," he said quickly, "it's not that. If you get tired of my company, then you'll need to say something, because…" He glanced toward the windows before looking at her again. "Because I haven't had such a good time in ages.…"

CECELIA DOWDY

has been an avid reader since she learned to string letters together to form words. While she pursued a business degree in college, one of her professors tried to convince her to get an English degree since he felt she was a great writer. Years later, after receiving her B.S. in finance, she took her former teacher's advice and started pursuing her literary career.

She loves to read, write and bake delicious desserts during her spare time. Traveling is another favorite hobby, and she's been to various countries around the world, including Germany, France, England, Tahiti, New Zealand, Mexico, Jamaica, Bahamas, the Cayman Islands and Santo Domingo. She enjoys listening to old tunes with her husband on Saturday nights. Currently she resides with her spouse in Maryland.

FIRST MATES

CECELIA DOWDY

Steeple
Hill®

Published by Steeple Hill Books™

If you purchased this book without a cover you should be aware
that this book is stolen property. It was reported as "unsold and
destroyed" to the publisher, and neither the author nor the
publisher has received any payment for this "stripped book."

STEEPLE HILL BOOKS

Steeple
Hill®

ISBN 0-373-87298-4

FIRST MATES

Copyright © 2005 by Cecelia Dowdy

All rights reserved. Except for use in any review, the reproduction
or utilization of this work in whole or in part in any form by any
electronic, mechanical or other means, now known or hereafter
invented, including xerography, photocopying and recording, or in
any information storage or retrieval system, is forbidden without
the written permission of the editorial office, Steeple Hill Books,
233 Broadway, New York, NY 10279 U.S.A.

All characters in this book have no existence outside the imagination of
the author and have no relation whatsoever to anyone bearing the same
name or names. They are not even distantly inspired by any individual
known or unknown to the author, and all incidents are pure invention.

This edition published by arrangement with Steeple Hill Books.

® and TM are trademarks of Steeple Hill Books, used under license.
Trademarks indicated with ® are registered in the United States Patent
and Trademark Office, the Canadian Trade Marks Office and in other
countries.

www.SteepleHill.com

Printed in U.S.A.

Thanks to my fellow writing friends,
Michelle Monkou and Loree Lough,
and to my best buddies Patty Elliott-Gray,
Alice Turner, Jay Briscoe and Alva Roane.

Hugs and kisses to my beloved husband,
Christopher Toomer, for always believing in me.

Much gratitude to my critique partners from
American Christian Romance Writers (ACRW):
Jennifer Johnson, Joy Libby, Flavia Crowner,
Rose McCauley and Amber Miller (Tiff).

My gratitude also extends to
Krista Stroever,
my editor.

Chapter One

Rainy Jackson peeked into the crowded dining room of the cruise ship. Stepping away from the entrance, she glanced down the empty hallway. Pacing down the hall, she ran her fingers through her hair. *What am I supposed to do now? Was traveling alone a mistake?*

Heavy footsteps pounded on the plush carpet. A voice, deep and masculine, resounded in the deserted foyer. "Hello."

She jerked toward the passenger, almost spraining her neck. While rubbing her collarbone, she gazed at the attractive man she'd seen earlier in the lounge. A warm smile graced his full lips as his presence filled the hallway.

Rainy tore her eyes away from the stranger, glancing into the crowded dining room again. She licked her lips before responding. "Hi."

His light-brown eyes seemed to pierce into hers. "Are you traveling alone?"

She touched her shorts. Should she have ironed them before coming to dinner?

After swallowing nervously, she nodded. "My best friends practically forced me to take this cruise."

He chuckled. "Really? My brother had to make me go on this cruise. He even bought my ticket." He paused as he continued to stare. "Did you want to eat together?"

She nodded. "Okay."

They entered the dining room and a waiter approached, clutching two menus. "Are the two of you dining together?" Rainy nodded and as she strolled behind her dinner companion, she watched his dark jeans hug his lean hips.

The waiter placed their menus on the table. "Enjoy your meal."

After settling into the padded chair, she slipped her shoes off and wiggled her toes in the plush cranberry-colored carpet. Photos of the aqua sea decorated the cream-colored walls. Voices droned in the dining room as contented travelers enjoyed their evening meal. "You know, I've never been on a cruise before. I was afraid of getting seasick. But I kind of like the gentle rocking of the boat."

He opened his menu. "Yeah, I know what you mean."

She tried to read her menu, continuing to steal glances at her dinner partner. Long thick lashes surrounded his hazel eyes. She sighed. *I could get lost looking into his eyes.* He looked up and their eyes locked. She quickly looked away. He chuckled. "What's so funny?" she asked.

He put his menu aside. "We're about to share a meal, and I don't even know your name." Tremors of delight coursed through her veins as he spoke.

"My name is Lorraine. Lorraine Jackson." They shared a firm handshake as he introduced himself.

"I'm Winston Michaels." She reluctantly released his hand.

"Everybody calls me Rainy, though." She pretended to study her menu.

The waiter returned to their table a short time later. "Would either of you care to order a drink? We have several wine selections to choose from."

He closed his menu. "I don't drink alcohol. Just bring me a Coke."

"I'll have the same." She gazed at her dinner companion with new respect. Could it be possible that he was a Christian, a child of God? Since her experience with her ex-fiancé, Jordan, it was hard for her to judge men. She slightly shook her head, dispelling the unpleasant thoughts about her recent breakup.

"Are you okay?"

"Uh, yes, why?"

"You seemed upset." Ripples of pleasure flowed through her as she gazed into his hazel eyes.

The waiter returned with their sodas. "Would you care to order now?"

She ordered the first item listed. "I'll have the fish and scallops."

"What side dishes do you want with that?" the waiter asked. He recited the choices and she made her selections.

Winston placed a straw into his drink. "That sounds good. I'll have the same." Once the waiter was gone, he selected a roll from the cloth-covered basket and slathered it with butter.

"So, tell me what a lovely lady like you is doing here all alone on this cruise."

She sighed, still trying to push the unpleasant memories away. "I've been through a lot the past few months, so my friends felt I needed a break. They insisted I take a vacation and soon enough, I agreed with them."

"Oh?" His expression turned curious. "Were you under a lot of stress with your job?"

She shook her head. "Honestly, no. Actually, work has been a good reprieve for me. I've never worked so many hours of overtime in my life as I have these past couple of months. I even brought some things to work on while I'm here."

"You brought work to do while you're on vacation?"

She nodded. "Yes, I have. I don't like to be alone for very long with nothing to do." She told him about her job in the accounting department of a prominent Miami newspaper.

"That's where you work?"

"Yes, I enjoy working with numbers. The accounting manager found another job, and since I was working so many hours anyway, I was the right candidate for the promotion." She told him about the trials and tribulations of running a successful accounting department. She was still talking when the waiter returned with their food. The aroma of steamed fish filled the air.

Winston bowed his head and Rainy lowered hers. *Lord, thank You for this wonderful meal, and thank You for allowing someone to share it with me. Please guide and strengthen both me and Winston during this cruise. Amen.* She opened her eyes and witnessed a smile soften his full lips.

She cut into her fish. "So why are *you* on this cruise alone?"

"Well, for the same reason as you. I've been through a lot over the past six months and my brother gave me this cruise as a birthday gift."

"When is your birthday?"

"This Sunday, the last day of the cruise. I'll be thirty-five." He frowned as he ate a potato.

"You're not looking forward to your birthday?" He wasn't very old, so she didn't know why he seemed to dread turning thirty-five.

"No, I'm not. How old are you?"

"I'm thirty."

"Thirty? I thought you were much younger than that."

She smiled. "People always say that I look younger than my age."

As they ate their meal, he continued their earlier conversation. "So, what happened? Why have you had to bury yourself in your work?"

She paused, finishing her entrée. "Let's just say it was a love relationship that went sour. That's all I want to say right now."

The waiter returned. "Would you like to order dessert?" They ordered chocolate cake.

She grinned as she tasted the first bite, enjoying the rich sweet confection. Curls of steam filled the air as the waiter poured their fragrant black coffees. She found the hot drink was a nice complement to their tasty dessert.

He placed his cloth napkin over the empty plate. "That was an excellent meal."

She drank her last drop of coffee and placed the china cup on the saucer. "It sure was."

"Do you want to go for a walk on the deck?"

"Sure."

As they walked on the deck, they passed other couples. They finally stopped as she gazed into the dark water. The waves crashed upon the ship and the obsidian sky twinkled with stars. "I can't remember the last time I've seen such a beautiful night."

He leaned against the railing and looked up at the sky. "It is nice, isn't it? Have you lived in Miami your whole life?"

"No. I'm from Maryland."

"Maryland? What are you doing in Miami? That's a long way from home."

She frowned as she toyed with her purse strap. "I love my parents and my family, but when it was time for college, I got a scholarship to a university in Florida and I was more than eager to leave. I was not too enthusiastic about life on the farm."

"So, your parents have a farm?"

"Yes. It's been in the family for two generations and my father loves it. It's a dairy farm so we've got tons of cows. I just didn't like all of the chores that had to be done each day. It takes a while to milk all those cows, even though we use a milking machine. Whenever I go home to visit, I always have to get used to the smell all over again. Have you ever been on a farm?"

"No, can't say that I have."

"Well, you're not missing much. My dad loves the animals and so does my brother Mark. He's already taken over a lot of the farm duties since my parents are getting older. Mark's married and he built a house on the property. I'm glad he decided to stay on the farm because my parents couldn't run it forever." Just thinking about the stench and labor on their dairy farm made her cringe.

"You hated it that much?"

She nodded. "Yeah, it was pretty awful. I hate the smell of a farmer. My family didn't really take many vacations since we couldn't leave the farm in someone else's care for very long. So I didn't get to travel much growing up. As soon as I was eighteen, I was out of there."

As they continued their walk, she told him the most important thing about herself—her deep faith in God and her baptism when she was twelve. "My parents have always stressed that having a deep faith in the

Lord is important, especially in today's world," she remarked.

Plates of elegant fruits and cheeses adorned the tables on the upper deck for the midnight buffet. Flocks of passengers watched the crewmen as they created a large sculpture of a fish from a block of ice.

Winston selected a small plate of treats, and as they shared the snack, their fingers touched as they grabbed strawberries and cheese. Later, they resumed their walk.

As fatigue settled into her bones, Rainy suggested they visit the hotel coffee shop. As they continued their conversation, she noticed the velvety darkness gradually fading. "We've been talking most of the night!" She yawned and he suggested escorting her back to her cabin. "Hey, you've made me do all the talking. You didn't tell me anything about yourself."

He chuckled. "We can save that for another day." As she unlocked her door, he touched her arm. Tingles of delight raced up her limb and she accidentally dropped her room key. Winston retrieved it and pressed it into her palm. "Rainy, this has been the nicest evening I've had in a long time." He touched her face before he strolled down the hall.

She swallowed, clutching the doorknob. "Good night." She closed the door and paced her room, full of energy. She plopped onto the soft bed and selected a piece of fruit from the basket that her best friends, Sarah and Rachel, had sent her as a bon voyage gift.

She parted the curtains and gazed at the endless expanse of sea. As she finished her pear, she realized this was the first night since her breakup two months ago that she had not dwelled on her relationship with Jordan.

Her ringing phone interrupted her thoughts. After she dropped the pear core into the trash can, she lifted the receiver, wondering if Winston was calling her from his room. "Hello?"

"Hey, Rainy!" Sarah and Rachel's voices sounded over the wire.

"You guys, what are you doing calling me on this cruise? You know how expensive this phone call is!" She smiled, gripping the receiver, enjoying the sound of her best friends' voices.

Sarah chuckled. "We're at my house. Rachel is on one phone and I'm on the other."

"We just wanted to make sure you were okay," Rachel added.

"Girl, you sure were a basket case earlier. You looked like you were going to cry when we left you on that dock!" Sarah commented.

She could imagine Rachel nodding emphatically. "Yeah, girl. You sure were in pretty bad shape."

Rainy thought about how much she had been missing Jordan since their breakup. En route to the Miami cruise ship dock, Sarah had stopped at a light, and a tall, chocolate-brown man jogged past. He looked so much like her ex-fiancé Jordan she had to fight to stay in the car. She had pressed her hands together when he paused at the light. While running across the street, the jogger glanced at the car. She had frowned as she looked at the stranger, disappointed that her imagination was playing tricks on her again.

That had been happening a lot, her seeing a man and assuming it was Jordan. The second time it had happened was when she attended a gospel concert with Sarah and Rachel. She'd dropped her pizza and soda while grabbing the stranger's arm. He pulled away as Coke and food splattered on his white T-shirt. She muttered an apology as he disappeared in the crowd. Closing her eyes, she recalled the sweet memories of her ex-fiancé. But thoughts of his infidelity reminded her of why he was no longer in her life.

Rachel huffed through the receiver, bringing Rainy back to the present. "Don't zone out on us! I just asked you a question and you didn't answer."

Rainy shook her head slightly and sat on the bed, gazing at the fancy fruit basket. "I'm sorry. What did you say?"

"I asked if you received the fruit basket."

She continued to stare at the basket. "Yes, I got it. Thanks, it was sweet of you two to send it to me."

Sarah chuckled. "And you still haven't told us if you're okay. Will you be all right on that cruise all by yourself?"

Thoughts of her romantic evening with Winston Michaels filled her mind. "You two shouldn't worry about me. I'll be fine."

Sarah continued. "Well, I'm thinking about booking a cruise in the future. Are there any eligible men on the ship? I'm determined to find myself a husband."

Rainy rolled her eyes. "Oh, brother," she muttered.

Rachel grunted. "Sarah, some of us aren't as desperate as you are to find a man! Don't you know you need to find happiness within yourself before you go on some big manhunt?"

When Sarah and Rachel broke into an argument, Rainy knew it was time to end the call. "You two stop fighting. I think it's time for us to get off of the phone."

Their argument stopped and Rachel commented, "Well, we don't want to keep you, girl. We'll say a prayer for your safety and be sure to call us when you stop at your ports of call."

Rainy said goodbye to her friends, touched that they were so concerned about her safety during this cruise. She replaced the receiver on the cream-colored phone. Nostalgia filled her soul as she realized she really did miss her friends even though she'd only been gone for less than a day.

She again thought about the evening she'd just spent with Winston. She removed her journal from the desk drawer and wrote about Winston Michaels and about the cruise. Her fingers flew across the paper, as words flowed from her hands, describing her curiosity about Winston and her desire to know everything about him. She stopped writing suddenly, gazing at the cream-colored walls.

I feel like I opened myself up, and told him all kinds of things about me, but he made no effort to tell me about himself. Could Winston be hiding something from me?

Chapter Two

"Come on, Winston, let's trick her again!" suggested Pam. Winston was seven years old, and Pam's mischief was in full swing that day. He nodded and they hid while his mother called their names. They jumped out of the closet. *"Boo!"* they yelled.

"Come out of there!" Their mother glared at them as they scrambled out of the closet.

Cold rivulets of sweat dripped down Winston's forehead as he awakened. He blinked and stared around the small unfamiliar room, baffled. His heavy breathing slowed as the gentle sway of the boat calmed his frazzled nerves.

Memories of boarding the cruise ship the previous day crashed his mind as he pushed the quilted comforter from his sweaty body. He stood on his shaky legs as he willed his muddled mind to awaken. Pam continued to plague him in his dreams, and he wondered when he would be able to sleep through the night.

While engulfing deep breaths of air, he stretched. He plodded to the closet and removed his carry-on suitcase. He dropped it onto the bed and opened it. The caramel-colored bottle of Scotch remained nestled among the folds of his garments. His dry, parched throat could use a sip of cool sweetness, and nothing would taste sweeter than a drink of Scotch. He licked his lips as he continued to stare at the enticing bottle.

The alcohol had been a bon voyage gift from one of his co-workers. All of his friends and acquaintances knew he didn't drink alcohol, but sometimes a person or two did forget about his beliefs. He removed the bottle and opened it. His lips were inches away from the nozzle, and he inhaled deeply.

Clutching the bottle, he walked into the bathroom and poured the rich brown liquid down the toilet. The sound of it flushing away gave him an odd sense of relief and sorrow. Trudging back into the bedroom, he placed the empty bottle on his dresser. *Since Pam's death I'm finding it harder to stick to my sobriety vows. Jesus, help me.*

He opened his heart and mind to the Holy Spirit. Tension eased from him as he gazed at the weak sunshine sifting through the window. Enjoying the warm glow, he turned toward the clock.

"It's so early," he mumbled. *I wonder if they serve breakfast at seven o'clock on this ship.* As he pulled cruise ship brochures and pamphlets from the desk drawer, he forced his near-slip from his mind, causing him to remember his late night with Rainy Jackson. She was a breath of fresh air!

Entering his bathroom, he took a long, hot shower. He dressed in the first pair of swimming trunks and T-shirt he found in his drawer. Minutes later, he walked the length of the dining room and scanned the tables, surprised that a lot of elderly couples were already up, enjoying their meals.

Where was Rainy? His stomach growled as he finally spotted her sitting alone. She was eating a toasted bagel and a plate of fruit while she read a book.

"Hi there." He sat beside her and watched her mouth perk into a smile.

"Hi, yourself. What are you doing up so early?" She glanced at her watch. "If my estimate is correct, you only had a few hours of sleep, like me."

Frowning, he recalled the vivid dream that had awakened him so early this morning. He pushed the disturbing thought aside as he focused on the cart of pastries, cheeses and fruits being presented to him by a passing waiter. After he had a plate of food and a cup of coffee, he said a brief prayer before answering her question. "I just woke up and couldn't go back to sleep. I didn't really expect to find you down here. Besides, I could ask you the same question."

She shrugged, taking a sip of her coffee, before responding. "I woke up just like you. I had a nice conversation with my friends before I went to bed."

"Oh? I'm assuming you're talking about the ones who made you go on this cruise?"

She nodded, smiling. "Yes, they called to check in. I miss them."

"Have you been friends with them for a long time?"

"I met them in a Christian social group in college. We're more like sisters than friends." She continued to tell him about Sarah, who was on a constant manhunt, and about Rachel, who was always having problems paying her creditors. "They disagree and argue a lot, but I've gotten used to that." She mentioned that both of her friends had been baptized while they were still in college. "I was glad I was able to see them accept Christ. One thing we do share is our deep faith in the Lord. We make sure we spend time together regularly. We even eat lunch together once a week. Do you have any close friends, Winston?"

Frowning, he popped a piece of cantaloupe into his mouth and chewed, recalling the good friendships he had made through his Alcoholics Anonymous support group and the buddies he had in his church home. Not wanting to reveal too much to Rainy about his problem, he told her enough to satisfy her curiosity. "I've got a few friends through my church who are pretty close to me. I'm also pretty close to my brother, Deion. Even though he's my brother, I still consider him to be a friend, too." He pointed to her book. "What are you reading?"

"Just a novel I picked up at the gift shop. I was in such a hurry packing, and I had so much on my mind, that I forgot to pack something to read for this cruise."

He finished his coffee, signaling the waiter to refill

his cup. "Speaking of cruises—" he pulled out a sheaf of papers from the pocket of his swimming trunks "—I was wondering if you've made plans about what you'll do during this weeklong cruise."

"Do?"

He waited for the waiter to fill his coffee cup before he continued. "Yes, I'm talking about activities. We won't be returning to Miami until this coming Sunday, so we've got six more days of fun before we get home."

She nodded, as her pretty eyes glanced at the glossy brochures. "When you say home, I'm assuming you mean Miami? Is that where you live? I told you yesterday that I work downtown at the Miami newspaper."

"I've lived in Miami most of my life."

Together, they scanned the ship's itinerary. Today they were at sea, but tomorrow they were docking in Cozumel, Mexico. "Have you ever been there?" he asked.

"I've been there a couple of times. Once our church group sponsored a trip to Mexico and we stayed in Cozumel for a few days." She told him what she remembered about the place as he read the list of Cozumel's attractions.

Rainy picked up the itinerary and read the rest of it aloud teasingly. "Day four, at sea, day five, dock in Grand Cayman, day six, dock in Jamaica—day seven is the last day we'll have at sea before returning to Miami."

He chuckled as she placed the papers on the cloth-covered table. "Sounds like we're going to be having ourselves a nice trip. I've never been to so many places in such a short period of time."

"Me, either. This sounds like an adventure. I'm determined to just forget about everything and focus on having a good time."

Her dark brown eyes sparkled as she stirred her coffee. He wondered what in the world had happened in her soured love relationship that would cause her friends to force her to go on this cruise. He was tempted to ask, but she looked so happy, he didn't want to spoil this joyous moment by mentioning the bad experience she'd briefly told him about.

They sat in companionable silence as they finished their food. The waiter returned with the breakfast cart, asking if they wanted more, but they declined as they finished their coffee.

As the breakfast food settled in Winston's stomach, his fatigue returned. He stifled a yawn as he pushed his cup away. "You know, I was going to go on a swim at one of the pools this morning. But now I think I might go back to sleep for a few hours."

He watched her as she gathered her belongings and placed them into her large tote bag. "Well, I'm wide awake so I'm going to sit up on the deck and read for a bit."

"Okay." He made a note to look for her later when he did take his swim. He watched her lithe body as she exited the dining room. He then stifled another yawn before he trudged back to his cabin. The sunlight was now brighter as it spilled through the small round window. After changing into his nightclothes, he fell into a deep slumber.

Later that day, after a long nap, Winston returned to one of the pool areas, eager to take his swim. He removed his T-shirt and was about to plunge into the water when he noticed Rainy lounging on a chair, wearing a one-piece black bathing suit. Her hair was twisted into a bun, and she was sporting a pair of sunglasses. She was reading a book and when she looked up and saw him, she dropped it on the floor. Smiling widely, he hurried to her lounge chair, sitting in the empty seat beside her.

"Hi." He lifted her book and when she took it, their fingers touched. Her skin reminded him of warm, soft butter.

"Hi, yourself. Did you have a nice nap?" She placed a marker in her book and set it on the table.

He sighed and ran his hand over his face. Feeling his stubble, he realized he hadn't shaved. "Well, about as well as can be expected. This boat is always rocking."

"Does that bother you? I can barely feel it."

"No, it doesn't really bother me. Sometimes I have trouble sleeping in strange places. Whenever I'm on a business trip, I always wake up in the middle of the night."

Rainy sat up in her chair and placed her chin in her hand. He could barely see her gorgeous brown eyes behind her shades. "That reminds me, you still haven't told me what you do for a living. You know all about me, but I barely know anything about you."

"Well, I work with numbers, like you do. I'm a financial analyst. I like it well enough. It's a job."

An orange beach ball crashed between them, knocking her iced tea off the small table.

A young girl approached and retrieved her ball. "Sorry about that." She ran back to the pool, her pigtails flying in the wind. A waiter appeared with a fresh glass of tea and cleaned the mess.

She sipped her drink. "It's so hot out here that I've had to drink a lot of liquids."

He wiped sweat from his brow. The clear blue water in the swimming pool rippled in the light breeze.

An Asian couple walked by, holding hands. She frowned and bit her lip.

"Sometimes you seem happy and sometimes you seem sad, Rainy. Why?"

Her hand shook as she sipped her iced tea. "I told you last night that I just ended a relationship." She paused as she placed her tea back on the table. "Well, that's not true. I didn't end the relationship, Jordan did."

"Oh?" He leaned back in his chair and listened intently while children's laughter rippled in the afternoon breeze. "If you want to talk about it, you can. I'm a good listener," he urged.

She removed her sunglasses, wiping away tears. He found napkins at an adjoining table and he pressed the paper squares into her palms.

"It just hurts so much. Sometimes I'm fine and I don't think about Jordan at all. Other times, Jordan will just pop into my mind suddenly. I just don't understand why it's taking so long to forget him."

She gripped her armrest and gazed at the sea. "I can't believe I'm acting like this in front of you. You're practically a stranger."

His fingers brushed her shoulder, wanting to offer her comfort. "Don't worry, I'm not trying to find fault with you. I can tell that you're hurting. Jordan's obviously a fool. You said last night this happened a few months ago?"

She nodded as she blew her nose.

"Well, that's not very long ago. It takes time to get over these things."

Children continued frolicking in the swimming pool, splashing tiny drops of water onto the passengers. She seemed to be thinking—weighing his words of advice. "Have you ever been in love?"

He sighed. "Yes, a long time ago. Things didn't work out between us. We were both young and in college. She joined the Peace Corps after she graduated. It's been years since I've heard from her."

He continued. "Tonya was my first love. Sometimes I wonder what would have happened if we'd gotten married."

"How long did it take for the pain to go away?"

He smiled fondly, remembering. "I don't remember. I do know it took longer than a couple of months. Just give it some time. I'm sure you'll forget all about Jordan soon enough."

He returned to his seat. "I know we've just met and everything, but I enjoy spending time with you." Her dark brown eyes widened at his remark. She leaned back into the chair and put her napkin aside.

"Winston—"

"No, you don't have to say anything. I just feel that there's a connection between us. I don't like seeing you sad. I think we should do something to get your mind off of Jordan."

She shrugged. "Like what?"

He chuckled. "Like having some fun. Why don't we play some games? There's lots to do on this ship to keep us busy, I'm sure." He helped her out of the chair and they walked to the shuffleboard game. A cruise director taught them how to play. Delight erupted in her laugh as she learned to ace the match.

Later, they sat in the Jacuzzi and enjoyed the rushing water as it tickled their brown skin. They visited all three pools on the ship so that Winston could swim his laps. Drinking fragrant cups of steaming coffee in the café, they watched the ocean view.

He ran along the lower deck, and she vowed to catch him. "You can't get away from me. I was a track star in high school." She flew down the deck, grabbing his arm as they shared a rich hearty laugh.

They stopped on the terrace as they enjoyed cookies for afternoon teatime. Rainy grinned as she gazed at the vanilla and chocolate cookies, coated with sugar. "These look great." She pulled a chocolate cookie from the tray. "They feed you an awful lot on these cruises!"

As he poured coffee, they watched the sea before munching on their snack.

The workout room was nearby, and he spotted a group of women sweating through an aerobics class. The instructor yelled so loud, he could hear her through the window.

Rainy eagerly selected another sugar cookie and sipped her coffee. She brushed the crumbs from her fingers and continued to grin. When they were finished with their snack, they returned to the pool. She dozed while Winston swam laps. When he was finished swimming, he grabbed a towel and headed toward her.

He wiped drops of moisture from his torso and arms as he walked to the rail. Two female Hispanic teenagers stood at an ashtray, smoking cigarettes. They gasped when he approached, and they scanned the deck as they hurriedly doused their cigarettes. They giggled as they raced to the pool and jumped into the water.

The rippling ocean sparkled beneath the bright sunlight. The view was so breathtaking, he was amazed and thankful that God created such beauty on this earth. He took a deep breath and grasped the railing.

Rainy stirred in her slumber. She opened her eyes and his heart pumped a steady rhythm as her gaze settled upon him. He strolled to her chair and touched her face. A thoughtful smile curled her shapely lips, and he wondered what she was thinking. "Did you have a good nap?" he asked.

She nodded. "How was your swim?"

"It was great. You know, we had such a good time at

dinner last night that I was wondering if I could enjoy your company tonight, too."

"I'd love to have dinner with you tonight." He touched her shoulder.

"Thanks," he whispered.

Chapter Three

Rainy rushed to her cabin late that afternoon. She opened her closet and scanned every dress before removing a few selections. The sapphire-blue dress would bring out the brown color in her skin. The silk taffeta was simple but striking. The cranberry dress looked good also. While chewing her lower lip, she finally made her selection.

Choosing the taffeta, she entered her bathroom and gazed at her reflection in the mirror. Piling her hair on top of her head, she wondered if she should sport a more sophisticated look for her dinner date. So many choices!

While showering, she thought about her day. This cruise was going to be so much fun! Sarah and Rachel had really done her a favor by forcing her onto this ship.

After drying herself with a white fluffy towel, she dressed for dinner. Upon opening her jewelry box, the first item discovered was Jordan's necklace. Her fingers touched the expensive freshwater pearls.

Would Jordan want her back? The sound of his voice as he called her from England, ending their engagement, scattered through her mind like unwanted weeds in a garden. *I can't believe he actually found another woman in a foreign country! He said he didn't want me, so do I even want him back?* She shook her head, dispelling further thoughts of Jordan. They weren't going to reconcile, and that was final. She replaced the necklace and slammed the lid of her box. The sound echoed in the small room. The only jewelry she would wear was a pair of earrings.

She forced herself to think of Winston as she placed the studs in her ears. Gazing at her reflection in the mirror, she sprayed her favorite jasmine perfume over her chest and arms before she finished dressing. The wonderful floral scent tingled her nose.

While pacing her room she glanced at the clock, finally sitting on the bed and continuing to wait. A hard insistent knock vibrated through the room. Seconds later she opened the door and gazed at Winston Michaels. His dark tuxedo accented his broad shoulders and trim waist. His silk shirt was a splash of ivory decorating his chest. Waves of nostalgia washed over her as she recalled her first high school party.

He touched his head. "I got a haircut. The barbershop was pretty crowded, but I convinced them to squeeze me in."

A warm glow radiated from his face as he looked at

her. "You look nice." *I'm glad I took the extra time in preparation for this special date.*

She returned his smile, hoping her voice wouldn't falter. "You look nice, too."

He cleared his throat. "I'm glad they have some formal dinner nights on this cruise. It gives us a chance to dress up." He chuckled softly. "I love having a pretty lady with a fancy dress on my arm."

Her heart raced with excitement as they strolled to dinner. The dining room was extravagant. Each table was decorated with white tablecloths and a vase of fresh flowers. The lights were dimmed, and the soft glow of candles permeated the room.

Most of the women wore formal dresses in different colors. It seemed as if a rainbow exploded and the shades randomly settled around the tables.

The waiter showed them to their seats. "You look nice tonight, ma'am." The waiter attempted to pull her chair out, but Winston beat him to it. She thanked him as she settled into her seat.

"You look so beautiful tonight," he mumbled as they opened their menus.

"Thank you." *That's the second time he's complimented me tonight.*

The waiter returned minutes later. "Our special tonight is filet mignon with baby potatoes." He took their dinner and drink orders before leaving the table.

Rainy smiled. "I find it hard to believe we spent the whole day together. We're acting like we just met."

Winston gazed around the festive room. Subdued

voices mingled in the background. "I know. The formal clothes, and the candles—" he tilted his head toward the lighted tapers "—make things seem different. But I'm the same guy who was wearing swimming trunks this afternoon."

She giggled and relaxed into her chair. "I'm glad we're having dinner together."

"Me, too."

The waiter returned minutes later with their food. He placed the dishes on the table and removed the silver covers. "Enjoy your meal."

He cleared his throat, looking slightly nervous. "Do you mind if we pray over our meal together?"

She nodded, pleased by his request. "I'd love to." She bowed and closed her eyes, listening to his strong voice as he thanked the Lord for the food and for this day of life. He prayed for their safety while on the cruise. He prayed for God to heal Rainy's aching heart. After saying "Amen" simultaneously, they started their meal.

The scents of juicy steak and buttery potatoes wafted through the air. The clinking of silverware against china filled the room as the other diners enjoyed their meals. After they had their apple pie and ice cream for dessert, they took a long walk on the deck. Several couples passed, still wearing their formal evening attire. A warm gentle breeze blew over the water.

Winston leaned against the railing. "You know we're docking in Cozumel tomorrow."

"Yes, I can hardly wait. I'm ready to get off this ship for a day."

"Would you mind if we spent the day together?"

She smiled and touched his muscular arm. He reminded her of a schoolboy asking for his first date. "I wouldn't mind at all. As a matter of fact, I was kind of looking forward to spending the day together tomorrow."

She was rewarded with his huge grin.

"You know, since both of us live in Miami, I think we'll be seeing a lot of each other once we dock," he commented.

They continued to stroll around the deck as the calm, soothing silence enveloped the beautiful night with tranquility.

Later that night, as they watched the comedy show, Rainy laughed so hard that tears came to her eyes. After the show, they returned to the upper deck.

Scents of luscious berries, fruits and desserts wafted around the deck as the crew prepared for the midnight buffet. As the workers carved a mermaid-shaped ice sculpture, Rainy prepared a plate of food and they sat at a table to enjoy their late snack. "I'm going to gain ten pounds by the time this cruise is over." She patted her full stomach.

He perused her from head to toe with his hazel eyes. "I don't think gaining a few pounds will hurt you at all." She flushed with pleasure. She sometimes worried about her weight and it was nice that Winston liked her appearance.

* * *

Early the following day, she met Winston for another breakfast date. As she slathered butter and syrup over her hotcakes, she caught him staring at her.

A fluttering ripple of butterflies seemed to move through her stomach. He quickly looked away, focusing on his plate of scrambled eggs and bacon. "What's the matter?" she asked before taking a bite of sausage.

"I'm just concerned that I'm monopolizing your time on this cruise. I know you came here to relax and everything and…"

She shrugged. "And what?"

"Well, I just hope you don't mind spending so much time with me. We barely know each other." He gazed at the other passengers enjoying their breakfasts. "This ship is full of people and I don't even think you've had the opportunity to mingle with the other guests."

I can't believe he seems to be on the verge of apologizing for spending time with me. A horrifying thought entered her mind. *What if he's only spending time with me because he feels sorry for me? What if he wants to be rid of me for the rest of the cruise so that he can meet other women?*

She sliced her fork through the stack of pancakes, but she'd lost her appetite. "Look, if you're having second thoughts about spending the day together—"

"No," he said quickly, "it's not that. I just don't want to make you feel like I'm pushing myself on you. If you get tired of my company then you'll need to say something, because…" He glanced toward the windows before looking at her again. "Because, I haven't had such a good time in ages. I'm glad I met you, and I enjoy your company."

Mentally sighing with relief, she gazed into his hazel eyes. "I'm glad we met, too. I'm looking forward to seeing Cozumel today."

After enjoying their meal, they boarded the small boat with other passengers for the short ride to Cozumel. The crewman announced the last boat returning to the cruise ship would leave at midnight.

They strolled the crowded port area, gazing into store windows. Natives walked the streets, speaking only Spanish. Rainy gazed at her surroundings in wonderment, knowing it would be impossible to see everything in one day.

She admired Winston's strong legs as she walked beside him. "I'm going to need to get a few things for some people at home," he said.

"Me, too. Why don't we go shopping first?" After they visited several stores, she checked her watch. "We've only been gone for a few hours, and I already feel beat." She clutched her bags of gifts as they continued to wander the streets. She pulled her gift list from her tote bag. Every name was crossed out except for one. Winston's name was the last one on the list. She crumpled the paper and when they passed a trash can, she threw it away. *I don't want him to know I'm buying him a birthday card!*

He entered a sandwich shop. "I'll get a few cold drinks."

"Okay, I'll be in there in a minute. I still have a thing or two to buy."

He chuckled as he entered the shop. "You've already purchased enough gifts for half the city of Miami."

She left him for a few moments and found a secluded gift shop. She found a pile of greeting cards and she flipped through them. A card with a striking picture of the ocean caught her eye. After reading the greeting, she decided it was perfect for Winston. The words were warm and simple and she was sure he would like it. After purchasing the card, she signed it and carefully placed it into her purse.

After she joined Winston in the sandwich shop, they decided to spend the rest of the day on the beach. They found a local man to transport them to the best swimming location. He recommended a shallow beach where they could play with the colorful fish. The local welcomed them into his car. The engine sputtered several times before it finally started.

Minutes later, they were transported to the most exquisite beach Rainy had ever seen. She removed her T-shirt and shorts and stepped into the gentle cool royal-blue water. The fish swam around her legs, and she opened a bag of stale bread she'd purchased from the shop and fed the small critters.

As the day progressed, she watched Winston slice through the water like an expert. A few times, she noticed his frown as he looked to the horizon.

Too soon, their romantic day was over. She closed her eyes as they took the boat back to the ship. She could barely lift her legs as she climbed the ladder onto the large boat. She noticed it was seven o'clock. "Dinner is casual tonight."

He touched her arm as he walked her to the cabin. "I'm glad about that. I don't have the energy to put on a tux tonight."

When she returned to her room, she took a long hot shower, hoping the water would soothe her aching muscles.

Winston's hard knock announced his arrival. "Hey, beautiful," he greeted. As they strolled to the dining room, they saw that the place was cluttered with passengers. The buffet was almost empty, and harried crewmen bustled from the kitchen with steaming trays to replenish the food supply. The noise level reached a deafening pitch, and Rainy wondered how they would communicate during dinner.

A server approached, leading them farther into the room. "We only have one dinner seating tonight instead of two. Just sit wherever you can. I'll be around to get your drink orders later."

They walked through the crowded dining area until Winston spotted a couple leaving a table. They plopped into the chairs. Another couple occupied the remaining two seats. After they got their food and said a quick prayer, they attempted to enjoy their meal. She struggled to stay awake as she ate her crab cakes and salad. She declined dessert, and Winston suggested strolling on the deck before heading back to their cabins.

Rainy sighed as they walked outside. She leaned on

the railing and stared at the dark sky. The moon was an ivory circle amid the blackness. Clouds floated by, enshrouding the moon with their shadows.

"Isn't it pretty?" she asked, tilting her head toward the sky.

"It's a perfect night. A wonderful end to a perfect day." As he escorted her back to her cabin, she yawned.

"Tired?"

"Yes. I know I'm going to sleep good tonight." When they arrived at her cabin, he caressed her cheek. Rays of warmth and passion clouded her fatigued brain, and she was reminded of the dangers of being alone with a man. She swallowed as she gazed into his hazel eyes.

"You have circles under your eyes. You need to get to sleep." He crowned her with a warm smile. "Good night."

She paused. "Good night." She watched him until he was no longer in sight. She closed the door and walked to her dresser. The boat gently swayed as she touched her cheek. She tried to remember the last time she'd been so happy. As she dressed in her pajamas, a frightening thought entered her mind. *The last time I was this happy was when I started dating Jordan.*

He'd romanced her like an expert. He took her to expensive restaurants. He showered her with expensive gifts and roses. He made her feel like a queen. However, that special feeling was burned to ashes. She still had his engagement ring in her jewelry box. She didn't even know the proper protocol about such things. Was she supposed to return the ring since she was no longer getting married? Jordan had not asked for the ring back, so she didn't know what to do with it.

Her fatigue lifted for a few moments as her anxiety returned. She wrote her confusing thoughts in her journal. She was concerned about her budding feelings for Winston Michaels. She was still upset about Jordan's betrayal. When she was finished with her journal entry, she lay on her bed.

She prayed to the Lord with her whole heart. She prayed for guidance in her friendship with Winston. She prayed for her memories of Jordan to disappear. She also prayed for the safety of her friends and family. She whispered "Amen" before she fell asleep.

The next day when Rainy awakened, she opened her curtain and gazed at the ocean view through her window. Rays of platinum sunlight filled her room with warmth. She still wasn't sure if Winston was the right man for her. She paced and considered her situation, running her fingers through her hair. She plopped into a seat as she made a decision. *I think I need to stay away from Winston for a few days. The last thing I need to do is to get deeply involved with him, only to have him hurt me the way Jordan did.*

She lifted the receiver and dialed a number. "Room service? I'd like to order French toast with maple syrup and a double order of coffee."

She replaced the receiver, still agitated. Maybe the coffee would clear the cobwebs from her brain. She barely tasted the meal, she was so preoccupied with her thoughts about Jordan and Winston. When she was finished, she changed into her bathing suit and packed her beach bag with her reading material.

She locked her cabin and walked the ship until she found a secluded lounge chair on the lower level. She lay down and closed her eyes as visions of Winston Michaels swam through her head. Heavy footsteps pounded on the gangplank, shaking her chair.

"Hi, beautiful." His gentle tone caressed her ears. Her eyes fluttered open and she surveyed Winston from head to toe. He sported a pair of pale blue swimming trunks and a beige T-shirt emblazoned with "Cozumel" in black letters.

She blinked, trying to clear her foggy brain. "Are you going to the pool?" she asked as she started to smile, before recalling the decision she made earlier. She quickly looked away.

Winston scratched his head, baffled. Rainy Jackson was a woman of mystery. If he didn't know better, he would have thought she wasn't happy to see him. "What's wrong?" He sat in an empty chair.

"Nothing," she spat, toying with the book in her lap. "I just really need to be alone today."

He hesitated, running his hand over his face. "Oh, okay." He stood and continued to stare at her tight-lipped expression. "Bye." He stomped away so fast he almost fell on the wooden deck.

Minutes later, he dove into the swimming pool. He pumped his arms through the water, swimming as hard as he could. He pushed himself until his arms were aching for rest. He tried to erase everything from his mind as he drove his body to exhaustion. *I can't do this anymore!*

He stopped and climbed the steel ladder out of the pool. He gasped huge gulps of air as he grabbed a towel and hobbled to a lawn chair. Once his breathing returned to normal, he toweled the water from his body. The scorching sun matched his hot, angry mood. He signaled a waiter and ordered a large glass of water and a glass of iced tea. He gulped both beverages and ordered two more.

A feminine voice tinkled in the hot humid air. "I'm surprised to find you here alone." His gaze traveled over the shapely cocoa-brown woman as she sat in the vacant chair beside him. Her black-and-white striped bikini hugged her physique like a second skin. She smiled and fluttered her lashes, her large dark eyes probing into his.

"I'm Carol." She presented her hand, showing long, red, talon-like nails.

He accepted her hand. "I'm Winston."

"Winston. That sounds like a nice strong name." She continued to stare. "And you look like a nice strong man." She pulled some sunblock out of her large bag. "I saw you swimming all those laps in the pool. You swam like Satan himself was after your soul. I just love it when a man is fast at doing physical things." She popped the top on her lotion and poured a generous amount into her palm. "So tell me, where's your girlfriend this morning? I was starting to think you two were joined at the hip."

"Excuse me?"

She giggled as she slowly rubbed lotion over her flat abdomen. "You know, the woman you've been with over the past few days. I've been dying to introduce myself, but she's always with you. I haven't had a chance to speak with you until now. She's not coming anytime soon, is she?" She stopped rubbing the lotion as she gazed around the deck, her dark eyes full of anxiety.

"It was nice meeting you, Carol, but I really need to get going." Carol's silence was rewarding as he took his exit.

Rainy pushed her book aside. "Oh, what have I done?" Winston's hazel eyes had flickered with pain when she made her announcement. A cold knot of guilt settled into her chest, and she was anxious to remove the burden. Her hand flew to her mouth as tears coursed a smooth path down her cheeks.

Lord, help me with this pain. When her breathing calmed, she signaled a waiter for a glass of ice water and napkins. He placed the large frosty glass on the table. She drank the water and pulled several napkins from the holder. She blew her nose. "I need to find Winston," she mumbled as she stood.

She hurried to his favorite swimming pool, gasping when she witnessed a beautiful woman chatting with him. Rainy strutted away so fast, she barely noticed the passengers in her path. She returned to her secluded hiding place and reclined on the white deck chair. As she closed her eyes, the ocean breeze whispered over the ship and she relaxed. Shadows of sadness filled her mind as she drifted away into blessed sleep.

Chapter Four

As Winston abandoned Carol, he walked on every level of the ship, carefully avoiding Rainy's secluded hiding place. He finally found a secluded spot of his own. The nursery overflowed with energetic children. Several blocked his path as they invited him to a game of hide-and-seek. He plodded through the nursery and entered the empty discotheque. A lone waiter stood behind the counter. "We're not open yet."

He waved the comment away. "I just want to sit for a minute." *I know Rainy wouldn't dare come into this place.* The floor was streaked with dark marks and dirty cups, and glasses littered the tables. He sank in a vinyl chair and dropped his head in his hands, closing his eyes. The boat swayed as they made their way to their next destination.

"What's wrong with Rainy?" he muttered. He opened his eyes and enjoyed the cool dark air-conditioned room.

A group of Hispanic teenagers entered the discotheque, chattering in their native tongue. They regarded him with curiosity before they haphazardly moved glasses and cups, seemingly searching for a lost item. He sighed as he relaxed. He finally stood and exited the deserted discotheque. Everything would be just fine between him and Rainy Jackson. It just had to be.

Weak sunlight spilled into the room as Rainy awakened the following morning. She blinked, forcing herself out of bed. She was tormented with dreams about Jordan, awakening every hour. She plodded to the bathroom and gazed at her face in the mirror. She looked awful! Her eyes were red and puffy and her throat felt as parched as a desert.

Brushing her teeth, she recalled the itinerary for the day. They were docking in Grand Cayman, one of the most popular islands to visit. She looked forward to seeing this exquisite place in spite of her sadness. She changed into her bathing suit and packed her bag. She groaned as she left her cabin, fatigue settling in her bones. She pictured herself on the beach, napping all day. Her lips curled into an anticipatory smile.

She trudged onto the empty deck. She paced and glanced at her watch. Where was the first ferryboat to Grand Cayman? Minutes later, passengers flooded the deck. She scanned the crowd and was glad she didn't see Winston.

After she boarded the ferryboat, she removed her book from her bag and tried to read. Passengers chatted as the motor started. Someone sat beside her. She scooted to give the passenger more room. "Hi, there." Her heart skipped a beat as she gazed at Winston. His presence was like a spark of light on a dark day. He gave her a sad smile. "You look sleepy."

"What are you doing here? I didn't see you before I got on the boat." With shaky hands, she placed the book in her bag and removed her sunglasses. She placed the shades over her eyes.

"I was the last person to get on just before the ferry left. I guess you didn't see me. I really need to speak with you. Can we go someplace for breakfast when we dock?" Pain, raw and fresh, glittered in his hazel eyes, and she couldn't refuse his request. Visions of the beautiful lady at the pool cluttered her mind. Did Winston really want to continue spending time together on the cruise, or was this just an act? Was he already on a quest to find another date for the remainder of the trip?

The ferry stopped and clusters of people disembarked. They were the last patrons to exit the boat. "Please have breakfast with me," he pleaded.

She sighed, rubbing her back. *I'm so hot and tired!* "Okay."

Passengers cluttered the sidewalk, gazing at natives hawking their wares. Children clogged the street, selling a wide range of merchandise. Rainy reached into her purse and purchased a cotton scarf from a toothless boy for a few dollars.

They walked in silence for several minutes before they stopped at a restaurant and ordered coffee and sweet rolls. She poured cream and sugar in her coffee before she sipped the fragrant beverage.

Winston brushed away a stray fly as he fixed his coffee.

Licking her dry lips, she gazed at the rich gooey cinnamon buns. Her heart pounded as he touched her hand. His light caress calmed her frazzled nerves. She relaxed as she gazed into his eyes.

"Rainy, please tell me what's wrong."

She closed her eyes, saying a silent prayer. She took a deep breath and told him how her apprehensions returned after they spent the wonderful day together in Cozumel. "I had not felt that happy since I'd dated Jordan. Everything seemed to be moving so fast and I just needed some time alone."

"I see." He gazed at the table, toying with a napkin.

"I didn't mean to hurt you. I just felt so confused."

"You shouldn't judge every man you meet just from your experience with Jordan. Not all men would treat you that way, especially a Christian man."

She sipped her coffee and placed her cup back on the table. "That's what I wanted to talk to you about."

He continued to give her his attention.

"I wanted to know if you were really a Christian."

He turned away. "I told you I was a Christian the first night we met. Are you asking me if I was lying to you?" His voice wavered with anger and hurt. The server turned the music louder as he danced to the Jamaican tune while wiping the counter.

She barely glanced at the server as she abandoned

her meal. "So many people in this world profess to be Christians, but then it turns out to be just talk."

He sighed and ran his hand over his clean-shaven face. "Why are you asking me this now?"

She nervously stirred her coffee. "When I first met Jordan, I could tell that he liked me. When I invited him to my church and told him how I had accepted Christ as my Lord and Savior, he said that he had done the same thing." She paused as she put her spoon aside. "Anyway, we worshipped together every Sunday and he even went to Bible study with me. When we broke up, he said he had done all of that just to please me. He said he'd acted the part of a Christian because he loved me so much and he knew how much I wanted a Christian man in my life."

He shrugged his broad shoulders. "You are a beautiful woman and you're intelligent, too. I'm not advocating what Jordan did, but I can understand why someone would go through such measures just to have a woman like you in his life."

She folded her arms in front of her chest, glaring at him. "But don't you think it's awful? Jordan claimed that he shared my faith and it turned out that it was all a lie."

He waited a few minutes, seemingly weighing his words. "Yes, what Jordan did to you was pretty awful. One should never profess a strong belief in Christ when it doesn't exist. I'm merely saying that a man will sometimes go through extreme measures when he cares about a woman."

"Jordan didn't care about me. He only cared about himself. He was a selfish and cruel man." Saying the words left a bad taste in her mouth. Winston stared, seemingly surprised by her outburst.

"So your boyfriend didn't care about you?" His voice was loaded with curiosity.

"I don't want to talk about it anymore. I don't want to ruin such a beautiful day talking about Jordan."

They continued to sip coffee and munch on sweet rolls. The server returned to their table and refilled their cups. As she ate her breakfast, she thought about Winston's advice.

He continued when the server left. "Relationships don't always work out. Sometimes you have to lean on God and pray for the strength and guidance to move on."

She sighed and rubbed her forehead. Did she even want to tell him more details about her relationship with Jordan? She certainly didn't want Winston's pity. God had blessed them with a glorious and beautiful day. The blue ocean sparkled under the bright morning sun, beckoning them to the pristine beaches. "Like I said before, I don't want to talk about my relationship with Jordan. I just want to let you know that it was more serious than just a casual dating relationship. That's all I'm going to say for now."

"Okay." He nodded and squeezed her hand.

"Another reason I've been avoiding you is because you don't tell me a lot about yourself. There's so much about you that I don't know. Sometimes I get the impression that you're hiding something from me."

"What did you want to know?"

"Well, remember when you said that I looked sad sometimes?"

He nodded.

"Well, I think you look sad sometimes, too, and I wanted to know why."

"I know I promised to tell you more about myself, and I will…soon. I want us to just have some fun on the island today." He paused, staring at a spot on the table. "I promise I'll tell you when the time is right. This is one of the most difficult times in my life and I'm having a hard time coping with the pain."

She squeezed his hand, wanting to give him strength. She felt bad about focusing so much on her own pain when he could be hurting just as much. "Did you just end a relationship, too?"

He shook his head. "No, it's nothing like that. I'll tell you about it soon," he repeated. "It's such a beautiful day that I don't want to ruin it by talking about something so sad." He looked away, and she thought she saw his hazel eyes glisten with tears. However, it was so quick that she wondered if she imagined it.

"I'm so sorry you're hurting." Her heart went out to him. "I just wish I could lift our pain and make it disappear." She sighed. "Only God could perform such acts. Maybe we should pray together. Nothing works as good as prayer when you're hurting." He nodded and took both of her hands.

His deep voice was calm and soothing as he prayed to their Heavenly Father. He prayed for guidance during their difficult time. He prayed that they could be lifted from their sorrows, if only for one day. Her soul felt cleansed as she squeezed his hand and said "Amen."

"Are you ready to have a wonderful day?" she asked as they stood and he left money on the table for the bill. He nodded and grinned as they walked out the door. She spotted the beautiful woman he'd been speaking to the previous day. She was giggling and flirting with an older man. When Rainy stopped walking, Winston gave her a questioning look.

"What's wrong?"

She stepped away from him. "I have something else that was on my mind." They stood on the sidewalk enshrouded among throngs of people. "I saw you on the deck yesterday talking to that pretty lady."

He looked puzzled as he gave her his undivided attention. "What pretty lady?" She again wondered if he was just putting on an act.

"You know, that lady on the deck."

Chuckling, he continued walking down the street. "What's so funny?" She planted her feet, refusing to walk any farther.

"You're funny. That woman was flirting with me. If you had stuck around long enough, you would have seen me leave her after a few minutes of small talk. Her name is Carol, and I think she came on this cruise to find a man."

"So, this Carol woman was flirting with you?"

He chuckled again. "Of course. Listen, whenever I travel alone I always have at least one woman proposition me for a date. Hey, I'm a good-looking man, so it's something you have to get used to," he said with a smile. But she couldn't get accustomed to women flirting with Winston. "I'm sure you have the same problem."

"No, I don't."

He continued to smile as she gazed at him. "Yes, you do. Haven't you noticed the men ogling you since we've been on this cruise?"

"They have?" She furrowed her forehead as they continued to walk. "No, I guess I haven't noticed."

"Well, I have. Do you know what I was worried about when you said you needed a break for the day?" They turned a corner. She barely noticed the throngs of people as they passed by. She was in a secluded world with Winston.

"What?"

"Well, I was worried that you would find another companion. I thought you wouldn't want to see me anymore during the entire trip." He stopped walking and gave her an intense look. She breathed the humid summer air, trying to calm her thudding heart.

"I don't think you realize just how beautiful you are. We've been on this sidewalk for close to fifteen minutes and two men have already taken a second look at you. I am very glad to hear that you were jealous to see me with Carol."

Her lips curved into a smile. "Why?"

"Well, since you were jealous, it at least shows that you care about me and about our friendship."

He continued, "And when we dock in Miami, I plan

to continue seeing you, that is, if you have no objections."

She smiled, gripping the handle of her purse. "I definitely have no objections."

"Let's just have a good time today, okay?"

She nodded eagerly, looking forward to the day.

A cab escorted them to the beach and she enjoyed the warm sand swishing through her toes as they walked the shoreline. Being with Winston wrapped her with warm wonderful feelings. Feelings she hoped and prayed would develop into something beautiful. She opened her camera and caught Winston's essence on film.

All too soon, evening arrived. He unzipped his backpack, producing two tickets to a sunset buffet. "Do you want to go?" He waved the slips of paper in the air.

"Are you sure we'll be back in time to board the boat?"

Grinning widely, he tilted his head toward the ticket booth. "I've already checked things out while you were laying on the beach. We'll be back in plenty of time to get back on our boat. I've already made all of the arrangements."

Hours later, they entered the restaurant with several couples. An open bar graced the reception area and mouthwatering Cayman foods were arranged in elaborate crystal bowls. Her stomach growled, reminding her she had not eaten since breakfast. She piled her plate with fresh crabmeat, lobster, rice and potatoes. Luscious fruit-filled desserts topped their meal. Rainy was about to enjoy her first bite of strawberry pie when Winston placed his hand over hers. "No, don't eat that yet."

"Why?" As she held her fork in midair, she wondered if he'd lost his mind.

"Because I've been wanting to do something since I first met you, but I've been too embarrassed to ask."

"Well, what did you want to do?" Her mouth watered for her strawberry pie. Layers of fresh berries and cream cheese were encased in the piecrust.

"I want to feed you."

Her eyes widened as she gazed at the other people sitting on the boat, enjoying their meal. "Feed me? Why?"

He shrugged. "I know how much you want that pie, and feeding it to you will make me so happy."

He removed the fork from her fingers before feeding her the first bite of luscious pie. She closed her eyes and enjoyed the sweet, tangy flavor. Winston relished the next bite. Back and forth they enjoyed the sweet treat until the fork scraped the crumbs from the plate. With a large ivory napkin, he brushed the crumbs from her lips. They then strolled to an outdoor deck.

The glowing sun dipped in the sky, turning the luminescent day into fading twilight. He placed his arm around her waist as they watched the horizon.

As the golden globe finally dipped over the horizon, she closed her eyes, basking in the happiness of being with Winston.

Soon, they walked back to the beach. Rainy's footsteps were weary as they managed to find the last ferry to the cruise ship.

Passengers' voices chimed with delight as they talked about their day, the velvet blackness of the sky a testimony to the late hour. Rainy and Winston's silence was filled with peace and comfort.

After they entered the deck of the cruise ship, Rainy walked around, suddenly full of energy. "I guess I shouldn't have had all that coffee during dinner. You know there's no midnight buffet this evening."

"Did you want to spend the rest of the evening together? We could sit on deck and have something to drink."

"That sounds like a good idea."

"Why don't we go back to our rooms and drop our stuff off," he suggested. "I'll walk you to your room first." She nodded. They walked to her room, and she dropped her beach bag into her room and then she accompanied Winston to his room. She followed him into the cabin, anxious to see his private quarters. As soon as she entered she saw the empty bottle and she stopped, shocked.

"Winston, what's this?" His smile melted as she lifted the empty liquor bottle.

Chapter Five

Winston cringed as she gazed at the empty liquor bottle. Rainy's mouth dropped open as she fingered the thick container.

"Winston?"

"I think you'd better sit down. It's going to be a long night." He pulled out a chair. After she sat, he opened a large bottle of water. He poured the beverage into foam cups.

She leaned her elbow against the desk, cupping her chin in her hand. Had God led her to this room tonight to show her that Winston was a phony Christian like Jordan?

"I know you're probably upset and surprised, but could you just hear me out? Promise me you won't pass judgment about anything until I'm finished speaking, please?" His hazel eyes were full of warmth and compassion, and she forced herself to open her mind and heart, and listen to his words.

"I know I haven't told you a lot about myself since we've been on this cruise. I know all about you and your life on the farm. You've told me about how you came to accept Christ when you were twelve." He paused and stared through the window.

"When I went away to college, it was the first time I'd ever lived away from home. I was nervous. I just wanted to continue to make good grades in school and I missed my folks." He sipped his water.

"Well, when I was away at college, I found that I was nervous before exams. My roommate suggested that I try having a few drinks before I studied the night before a test. I was never a drinker before because my parents forbade it. However, I went ahead and tried his advice once. I found that the alcohol did relieve some of my anxiety."

He paused for several seconds before continuing. "Anyway, from that moment on, I found that whenever I wanted to drown my pain and sorrows, I drank alcohol. Remember that woman I was involved with, the one I told you about earlier on the cruise? I'd mentioned that she joined the Peace Corps."

She nodded. "You said her name was Tonya."

"That's right. Well, I started drinking even more after she left. I managed to graduate from school and start working, but it took me a while to admit that I had a problem and to do something about it. I joined Alcoholics Anonymous and I started to lean on God. During my college years and a short time after that, I had almost abandoned God and I paid for it. I fell by the wayside. But then I joined a church in the area in which I'd relocated and I visited my pastor." He finished his water and he began to rip the foam cup into tiny pieces. "Anyway, Pastor Jake reminded me that we're all sinners. When we mess up, we just need to confess our sins and ask God to forgive us."

Winston continued to speak and Rainy continued to listen. He spoke of his battle against alcoholism and the trials and tribulations in his life where he felt he had no choice but to drink. He also revealed that due to recent circumstances, he'd been tempted with the solace of alcohol again.

Her mind was crowded with so much information that she thought her head would explode. Questions and concerns scattered throughout her brain so fast that she didn't know which to ask first. Weak sunlight spilled through the window, announcing the dawn of a new day. She rubbed her forehead, gazing at the bottle. "When did you buy the bottle of Scotch?"

He sighed. "I didn't buy it. My co-worker purchased it for me as a gift. I guess he didn't realize that I didn't drink. He gave it to me right before I made the trip to the ship." She sighed, running her fingers through her hair.

"Rainy, I know you're ready to go back to your cabin. You look tired enough to fall asleep on your feet. But before I walk you back to your room, I need to ask you something." He fumbled with the torn cup. Rainy gazed into his troubled hazel eyes and nodded for him to continue.

"I want to know if you're mad at me. I still want to date you and everything. I just hope what I've revealed to you tonight won't be the catalyst that'll end our spending time together." She abandoned her chair and sat beside him on the bed.

"I'm glad you told me about this. It just shows that you're willing to tell me the truth. As you said, we're all sinners and we need to admit to our transgressions and lean on God for support. It's hard being a Christian and living by God's rules, but with His help we can overcome our weaknesses."

He nodded. "Amen to that. Part of my problem with my alcoholism was that I did put God on the back burner, not relying on Him for support. I feel that my faith is so much stronger now."

She closed her eyes, sending a silent prayer to God to help Winston with his weakness. She opened her eyes and they shared a brief hug.

"How about you walk me to my room, Winston? I'm so tired."

"I know you are." Glancing around his small cabin, she was again reminded of the reasons why it was not a good idea to be alone with this gorgeous man for long.

"Come on." He helped her up, and they walked to her cabin. "I'll see you later on today." He gave her a small smile before she entered her room.

She took a long, hot shower. She washed away the dirt and sand accumulated during their daylong excursion on Grand Cayman. Lying between the crisp cotton sheets, Winston's testimony played in her mind. Relief flowed through her veins as she clutched her pillow. He trusted her, and she now knew he was a Christian. He had his struggles, but he now leaned on God to get him through the rough times.

Before sleep claimed her in its deep depths, she remembered another question she wanted to ask Winston. He said due to recent troubles he was tempted to drink again. She wondered what recent troubles he was referring to? Again she wondered why he was so sad. She needed to ask him all about this as soon as possible. She cared about him, and if he was going through a rough time, she wanted to be there for him as a friend.

The following day, the huge boat pulled into the port of Jamaica. The horn blew, announcing their arrival. Rainy breezed into the dining room in the middle of the morning and found Winston at their table, feasting on bacon and eggs. He signaled the waiter for coffee. "I can't wait to see the waterfall," he commented.

Her mind was still full of concerns about what he had revealed the previous day, but she decided not to bring up the subject for the time being.

A few hours later, they trudged over rocks as they trekked to the falls. As the sun shone on the clear water, diamond chips seemed to sparkle on the surface. Rainy stopped and snapped another picture.

Since she had not had a lot of sleep the prior night, she found herself struggling to stay awake as they tried to enjoy the beautiful scenery of the tropical island. She glanced at Winston throughout the day and noticed he was also having trouble staying awake.

As they conversed with natives and visited the gift shops, she saw him looking at some expensive Jamaican pottery. "Are you thinking about buying one of those?" The thick jugs were painted in dark bold colors and Rainy thought they would look nice as decorations in a living room.

"I might buy one for my mother. I haven't bought anything for her yet and I think she might enjoy this. She collects pottery."

He selected one of the containers and told the clerk to gift wrap it for him. "I think I'll have them ship it to my parents' house. I don't feel like lugging it back with me."

She gazed at his handsome profile, wanting to soak up as much information about his life as possible, like an eager sponge. "Do your parents live in Miami?"

He chuckled. "Not anymore." He named a small Florida town, a few hours' drive from Miami, where they now lived since his father had retired. "I want to send her this vase now so that my mom can receive it and enjoy it for a while before they take their trip."

Puzzled, she asked for more details. "What trip?"

"They bought one of those big trailer trucks and they want to drive around the country and see the sights."

"By themselves?"

He continued to grin. "Yeah. Since my dad's retirement, they've been acting like they're teenagers again."

He fondly shook his head. "I don't understand it, but as long as they're happy, I'm not going to worry about it."

He filled out the necessary paperwork so that the clerk could ship the item to his parents' home.

"I'm sure your mother will enjoy her gift."

He squeezed her shoulder. "I think she will, too."

"Do you miss your parents since they've moved?"

"A little bit. I used to drop by and visit often when they were still living in Miami. Now that they're farther away, I can't see them as much as I'd like."

"I'm sure they miss you, too."

He shook his head. "I doubt it. I get the feeling they just wanted to get away from everybody and be by themselves. Sometimes I think they forget about me and my brother Deion." He watched the clerk as she continued to wrap the vase. "As a matter of fact, I speak to my uncle Greg and aunt Gladys more than my parents."

"Really?"

He nodded, explaining that his uncle was his father's brother and he grew up spending a lot of holidays at their house with his family.

When they returned to the ship that evening, they stood on the upper deck and enjoyed another midnight buffet. The stars twinkled in the sky, and she realized that the following day would be their last full day aboard the cruise ship.

Winston awakened late the following day. The bright sunlight spilled into his cabin. As he lay in bed, he thought about what he had revealed to Rainy two nights ago. *I avoided mentioning our conversation yesterday, but I can sense that she has a lot of questions about my drinking problem.*

Rubbing his eyes, he finally struggled out of bed. Gulping a large glass of water, thoughts of the fattening meals served on the cruise entered his mind. While at home, he frequented the gym at least three or four times a week. The ship had a small gym on the first level, and during this trip he had not exercised even once.

He changed into his workout clothes and strolled to the gym. He would get at least an hour of exercising done before he indulged in a tasty lunch. Opening the door, he spotted Rainy on the treadmill.

A breath of air flew across her skin as the door swayed open. She groaned, wishing to be alone for her workout. A soft gentle smile curled Winston's lips as he entered the gym. His light-colored warm-up suit clashed with his cocoa-brown skin. "Hi, there." Selecting the adjacent treadmill, he threw his gym bag on the floor. "I'm glad we're the first ones in the gym this morning."

"Hi, Winston." Her disappointment disappeared like ice during a spring thaw. She smiled as she adjusted the speedometer.

He set the treadmill to his desired speed. "I didn't know exercise was part of your routine."

"Yeah, me and Jordan." She paused. "We used to go

running together all the time. I've missed my workouts since I've been on this cruise."

"I agree with you about that." His feet pounded against the running machine. Adjusting the controls of her treadmill again, she gazed around the gym. The room was small and it contained three treadmills, three StairMasters, a weight bench and a section set aside for aerobics. The alabaster walls and cool temperature made a comfortable workout atmosphere.

Soon she was running along with Winston. She ran five miles and Winston ran six and a half. She did toning and stretching exercises while he lifted weights. When they were finished with their workout, they poured cups of water from the cooler and sat on a mat. They leaned against the wall and drank their beverages. Moisture caused her outfit to stick to her skin like glue, and vivid thoughts of a long, hot shower played in her mind.

Winston's labored breathing slowly became steady. "So, did you sleep well last night?"

She nodded. "The ship lulled me to sleep." She paused and took another drink of water. "You know, I wanted to talk to you about what you told me a couple of nights ago. But I didn't bother mentioning it while we were in Jamaica yesterday." She sighed. "I did think about what you revealed to me. I've been thinking about it for the past couple of nights. I think it was brave of you to tell me about your experience, and I'm glad that you trust me."

"Thank you."

"But I did have another question that I wanted to ask you." She placed her empty water cup aside. "I wanted to know what's been on your mind lately. You had said that you were tempted to take a drink the other day and that you poured the Scotch down the drain. Is something wrong? Did something happen to you recently?"

She watched him, wondering if he was okay. There were times after her breakup with Jordan when she was at the end of her rope. However, with the support of her church family, and prayer, she found that she could cope with such a devastating disappointment.

He dropped his cup on the mat. "Yes, as a matter of fact something did happen to me recently. It happened six months ago." She wiped her sweat with a towel as she waited for him to continue.

"I lost a family member six months ago."

"Oh? Somebody died?"

He nodded. "It was my twin sister, Pam."

She gasped, clutching her cup. "I'm so sorry, Winston. What happened?"

"She died of cancer. This Sunday will be the first birthday I'll be spending alone without her. That's why my brother Deion gave me this cruise as a gift. He knew how hard my first birthday without her would be."

"Oh, I honestly don't know what to say." She wondered how to offer her warmth and comfort. "I guess you two were pretty close?"

He nodded. "I was real close to my sister. We used to get into a lot of mischief while we were growing up, and she initiated it most of the time." He chuckled, his hazel eyes twinkling with warmth. "I still think about her a lot, and I dream about her, too. That was why I almost had a drink a few mornings ago. I had just had another dream about Pam. I just feel so sad sometimes. It just overwhelms me. I'm learning to deal with the pain, though. I'm not hurting nearly as much as I was six months ago."

"Is there anything I can do to help?" Her fingers caressed his cheek.

"No, there's nothing you can do. Just sitting here and talking and listening to me is enough. I feel comfortable enough to tell you about this. Thanks for listening to me." He squeezed her shoulder.

He continued. "I've had my share of disappointment over the past six months, and I'm dealing with it one day at a time. I'm leaning on God, and that's helped."

"Does your church offer grief counseling? My church does. Perhaps you could go to some of the sessions. They might help you to deal with your grief."

He sighed. "Yes, they do, but I just didn't feel comfortable talking about Pam in front of all those people. My memories of my twin sister are personal. As a matter of fact, you're the first person outside of my family with whom I've so openly discussed my twin's death."

"I'm glad you told me."

"I'm glad we're spending time together on this cruise. When I'm with you, I forget about my worries, for a little while, anyway."

Her heart lilted with delight. "I'm glad you feel that way."

A group of passengers entered the gym, anxious to begin their morning workout. They ran to the treadmills and set the controls while others lifted weights. Winston assisted Rainy to her feet and they left the gym.

After showering, they met near the grill area beside the pools. Rainy's stomach ached with hunger. "I guess I shouldn't have skipped breakfast before working out." They feasted on hot dogs, hamburgers, fries and sodas.

Winston finished his second burger. "This is great food."

The golden rays of sun disappeared behind angry gray clouds. The wind blew over her damp skin and she huddled under a towel.

"Looks like rain," said Winston as he gazed at the dark clouds gliding through the sky.

Other people abandoned their seats as the first drops of cool rain splattered the deck. Rainy and Winston quickly ran into the adjoining activity room. Flocks of passengers occupied tables and waiters scrambled to deliver drinks and refreshments.

Winston squeezed her shoulder. "I'll be right back." Walking to a shelf filled with games, he chose one. Vivid memories of games with her brother Mark crowded her mind as Winston set the pieces on the board. They threw the dice, moving tiny pieces to expensive properties. She enjoyed the buttery richness of the cookies served, and she drank fruit punch and soda as they played the intense game.

Music blared from the speakers as more passengers

crowded in the room. The buzz of conversation sounded in the background as they continued their game. "I won!" Rainy declared. Poking multicolored money in his face, she gloated.

"Don't get smart! I'll get you next time."

The rain finally stopped and the remainder of the day passed in a whirlwind of activity. She frantically tried to pack as much adventure into the small amount of time they had left on the ship. While spending time with Winston, she discovered little things about him. He loved his steak well done. He was passionate about his job and he hated the financial situation of lots of African-Americans. "It's just a shame that so many African-Americans are not taught good budgeting and investing skills," he admitted later that day.

Winston played in the ship's Ping-Pong tournament. He earned first prize—free pictures from the photo gallery. The ship's photographer had followed passengers like a shadow during the cruise, taking candid shots. Rainy and Winston walked to the gallery to choose which shots they wanted for the prize. "I can understand what you mean about the financial situation of African-Americans," she said, gazing at the photos. "I want to do a series of workshops for the teens at my church about that subject."

He glanced through the pictures lining the walls. "Really? When are you doing this?"

She giggled. "You know how things can be when dealing with church folks. Things have been disorgan-

ized at my church lately, and so far I haven't found anybody to help me with the project. I don't think I can
handle it by myself."

They continued to scan the walls of pictures. "Really? Well, I'd be more than happy to help. I've always
wanted to try to do something like that for the community. I think it's a good idea." He paused and brushed
her shoulder. "You've got a pretty good head on your
shoulders." His deep voice was like a caress and waves
of pleasure swiped through her as she enjoyed the enticing scent of his cologne.

He pulled a photo from the shelf. "Hey, look at this
one." She gazed at the candid shot of their dinner date.
Their profiles glowed as they leaned toward one another at the table, before starting their meal. Rainy
couldn't recall the last time she'd looked so pretty in a
picture. "I think I'm going to have extra copies made
of this one. I'm going to always keep this picture," he
promised.

She stepped away and gave him a guarded look. "Do
you really mean that?"

"Sure. I'm going to show it to my brother as soon as
we get to Miami. And the next time I visit my parents,
I'll show them, too." His hazel eyes glowed as he
looked at her.

Finally, too soon, evening arrived. Rainy strolled
through a myriad of passageways and stairwells as bittersweet memories of her first cruise played through her
mind.

As couples strolled along the ship, she realized how

much Winston had monopolized her time. He was the sole passenger she'd met at sea, and she didn't get a chance to mingle with other passengers.

Later that night, she pulled several colorful dresses from her closet. Scrutinizing each selection, she decided on the most appealing dress in her wardrobe. After showering and dressing, she plugged in her curling iron while deciding on the most appealing style for her hair. When Winston knocked on the door, she moved so fast, she almost burned her hand on the hot iron.

When she opened the door, he gave her a brief hug. "Are you ready?" he whispered in her ear.

"Aren't you a bit early?"

He released her and sat on the bed. "Nope, I'm on time." He pointed to the clock. "You only have a few minutes to get ready."

She returned to the bathroom and continued to curl her hair. "I'm sorry. I took my time getting ready and I wasn't paying attention to the clock."

"Why? You're always ready on time. You're not hungry for dinner?"

She took a half step into the bedroom. "I want to go to dinner and I don't want to."

He furrowed his brow. "Huh?"

"This is our last dinner on the cruise. We've had such a good time that I hate to see it end. But I am looking forward to spending the evening with you."

"Baby, don't ruin tonight by getting sad and sentimental on me. Let's just focus on having a good time.

But you'd better hurry." He pointed to the clock again, and she stepped back into the bathroom, resuming her preparations.

A couple of hours later, Rainy enjoyed the smooth creamy taste of the baked Alaska for dessert. Winston pried her fork from her fingers, feeding her the last bite of the succulent treat. Bittersweet nostalgia swept through her as she finished her last dinner on the cruise ship.

She sluggishly awakened as her alarm clock sounded early the next morning. Fat drops of rain splattered against her window as she exited the warm cocoon of blankets. An hour later she was refreshed and her bags were packed. She yanked the desk drawer open and removed Winston's birthday card. She caressed the ornate blue envelope. She clutched his card as she moved through the passageways. Minutes later, she took a deep breath and knocked on his door.

"Rainy!" He regarded her with curiosity as she stepped into his room. As she touched his elbow, his hazel eyes bore into her hers, relaying the pain and sorrow he suffered. "It's seven o'clock, so we should be docking soon."

"Yeah, I know." His leather bags, swollen with belongings, were packed and sitting beside the door. The familiar scent of his clean woodsy cologne dominated the small cabin. Black jeans stretched over his lean hips and his large feet were covered with pecan-brown sandals. Touching his muscular bicep, she swallowed and pulled the card from her purse.

"Are you okay?" she asked.

He shrugged. "About as well as can be expected."

She pressed the card into his hand. "Happy birthday, Winston."

"Oh, you didn't have to do this." Warmth and tenderness flowed through his voice.

"I purchased it while we were in Cozumel. I didn't know about Pam then. I didn't even know if giving you a birthday card would be appropriate in light of what you revealed to me. But I thought I'd take my chances and give it to you anyway."

He grinned as he opened the card and read it. "Thank you. I like it a lot."

"I'm glad I made the right decision. Are you sure you're fine today?" she asked again.

"I'm doing much better since you came to see me."

The bed creaked beneath their weight as they sat upon the blue comforter. He gave her a warm smile as he playfully tickled her stomach. Giggling, she sat in an upright position. He suddenly hugged her so tight, she wondered if he'd ever let go. "I don't think anybody has ever hugged me so hard."

"Well, hopefully I'll be hugging you a lot. I really like holding you, Lorraine Jackson." He held her chin between his index finger and thumb as his lips lightly touched her forehead.

He dropped his arms and opened the desk drawer. He pulled out a pad of paper and a pen. "Let's exchange personal information."

"Okay." Still swooning from his friendly kiss, she

wondered if she could write her information. She managed to place her phone number, home and e-mail addresses on the pad and he wrote his information on a fresh sheet of paper. "There's something else I wanted to ask you about."

"Yes?"

"Well, I don't expect you to say yes since we just got back home today and everything—"

He sighed and gave her a huge grin. "Stop beating around the bush and ask me."

"Okay. If you have time, could you come to church with me today? They have an evening service at six."

"Rainy, I'd love to go to church with you this evening." She wrote down the church's address, too.

"It would probably be best if we meet at the church at six o'clock this evening."

"I'll be there, sweetheart." He touched her cheek.

Chapter Six

Winston strolled beside Rainy as they left the evening church service and walked toward her car. Clusters of parishioners flowed out of the small church, some of the women openly staring at him. *The women at Rainy's church sure are nosy!* Rainy managed to introduce him to a few of the church members before service started, but he couldn't help but notice the curious glances he received after the introductions.

He guided her away from the small crowd, giving them some privacy. "I'm not ready to go home yet. Let's go out for ice cream," he suggested.

"You're on. But after ice cream I'll definitely have to make my way home. I've got tons of laundry to do and then I've got to get ready for work tomorrow."

As they approached the car, her step faltered as she suddenly grabbed his hand and clutched it so hard that her long nails dug into his skin. Her chocolate-brown eyes widened when she spotted a tall man with a mustache and beard leaning against her vehicle. He wore an expensive business suit and sported a gold ring on his index finger. His skin was the color of hazelnuts and he stared at Rainy as he clutched a briefcase.

Tension filled the air as she squeezed his hand again. "What are you doing here?" she breathed.

"Who is this?" asked Winston.

The stranger glared at Winston. "It's none of your business who I am. Me and Rainy have things to discuss."

Darkness enshrouded the small parking lot and curls of steam rose in the humid air from the recent rainfall, lending the man a sinister appearance. Winston sensed this stranger was bad news, and he didn't want him around Rainy.

Winston stood in front of Rainy, blocking her from the stranger's view. "She obviously doesn't want to speak with you."

The stranger replied with authority. "This is none of *your* concern. I need to speak with her alone. We have unfinished business to discuss."

Winston stepped closer to the stranger, causing him to cringe. "You're not talking to her unless I'm around."

She grabbed Winston's hand. "It's okay. I'll talk to him."

"Who is this?" asked Winston again.

"It's Jordan." She spoke so softly that he could barely hear her. He squeezed her hand, taking a deep breath. This pompous, no-good, arrogant man used to be Rainy's boyfriend? He couldn't believe it.

"I refuse to leave you alone with him."

"No, I want to speak with him."

She suddenly released his hand as waves of sadness filled his heart. He sighed. "I'll be over here if you need me." He pointed toward a tree before he walked a few feet away, watching them as they spoke. Her body seemed to shake as she wrung her hands. Their hushed tones carried in the warm humid air.

While they were on their cruise, she failed to tell him *why* her boyfriend had broken up with her. *What in the world are they arguing about?*

Sparks of shock and confusion shot through her when she saw her former fiancé. He looked the same. The new gold ring on his finger gleamed in the darkness. "What are you doing here, Jordan?" she practically growled. The mound of pain he burdened upon her had yet to disappear. She continued to look at him as he rubbed his hands, his dark eyes full of anticipation.

"You look even prettier than the last time I saw you." He stroked her hair and she stepped away from his touch. "Remember how I used to compliment your hair? I always said it was soft as the finest silk."

She cringed as she continued to stare. She recalled taking him to the airport and walking with him to the international terminal. They'd shared a long passionate kiss before he'd boarded his flight. As his plane flew into the air, she waved goodbye before touching the beautiful ring gracing her finger. She'd planned on visiting London, but he was always too busy and overworked to accommodate her visitation requests.

"Just answer my question." She clenched her teeth and folded her arms. "What in the world are you doing here?"

He chuckled as he continued to caress her with his eyes. "My job assignment in London is over. That's why I'm back in town."

"Why are you here at my church? I know you didn't come to praise God."

Continuing to smirk, he touched her arm, but she slapped his hand away. "Don't you ever touch me again, Jordan Summers."

"Calm down. I know I messed up, but I'd like to tell you how sorry I am. That's why I came here tonight." He paused and studied his hands. "Besides, this is not *your* church. Remember you used to say that the House of God belongs to anyone who wants to worship."

In spite of the warm air, chills fluttered down her spine. Was he planning on attending her church from now on? "Why are you interested in praising God? You said you attended service and Bible study just to please me. The last we spoke, you said you weren't even a Christian," she spat. She clutched her Bible so hard she thought her grip would cut through the leather cover.

"I think we still might have a chance—"

"Just be quiet. I don't want to hear this, not now." Pain settled into her forehead and she rubbed her temple. As soon as she got home she would take some aspirin and go to bed. She leaned against the car.

He glanced at Winston before he continued. "Look, I see you've got a new boyfriend now, but what we had was special. I think we have a chance at happiness."

She opened her mouth and closed it. When she found her voice, she expressed her doubts. "Look, you need to stop this. I'm never going back to you. Besides, what happened to the woman in London? Are you here with me now because she dumped you?"

He looked at the cars leaving the lot. Before he could say another word, she turned around and walked quickly toward Winston.

Winston's firm tone brooked no argument as he glared at Jordan. "I think you'd better leave so that Rainy can get into her car and go home."

Fear glittered in Jordan's eyes as he opened his car and threw his briefcase inside. Minutes later, he sped away in his fancy sports car.

"I can't believe the nerve of him to want to speak to you," Winston began.

"I'm so tired. I just want to go home."

"Maybe we can still go out for ice cream?"

She rubbed her forehead. "No, not tonight." She gazed around the now empty parking lot. "I've lost my appetite."

"Okay." He looked into the darkness and sighed.

She touched his arm as he led her to her car. "I'll explain everything to you soon, but not now."

He nodded as she unlocked her door. "I'm going to follow you home in my car. I don't trust that guy."

She rubbed her temple again and started the ignition.

"Jordan isn't the nicest man around, but he's harmless. You don't have anything to worry about."

"Don't argue with me. I'm going to follow you home no matter how much you object."

Driving home, the sight of Winston's headlights in her rearview mirror brought her comfort. As she entered her house, he honked his horn. She turned on her lights and waved goodbye to him from her window.

She dropped her Bible on the coffee table, walked to her bathroom and opened her medicine cabinet. She poured a glass of water and swallowed three aspirin tablets before she returned to her living room and lay upon her jade-green couch. She sighed and closed her eyes. Settling into the soft cushions, she rehashed the evening's events. Jordan was determined to enter her life again. Why? She dozed, willing her headache to disappear.

When she awakened, she took a shower. The pounding water eased her stress. As she dressed for bed, she gazed around her room. Since her breakup, her dresser and desk looked bare, bereft of Jordan's pictures. She kneeled, resting her elbows on her blue comforter, sending her prayer to heaven, begging God to give her the strength to handle Jordan's sudden reappearance in her life.

Before she slept that night, she wrote in her journal. She recorded her thoughts about Winston, Jordan and the last few days of her cruise. She then turned off the light and fell asleep.

Could life get more complicated? After seeing Rainy safely home, Winston's head was still spinning as he pulled into his garage. As he exited his car, he smelled the enticing scent of chocolate.

An unexpected voice greeted him in the darkness. "Hi there, big brother."

Jumping back, Winston banged his derriere into his car. "What in the world? Deion, you scared me!" His keys clattered to the ground as he clutched his stocky younger brother in a strong embrace. "Where's your car?" He glanced up the street.

"I parked a few blocks away. Remember how you and Pam used to go off and play by yourselves, and I'd get mad? I'd always think up my own mischief, ways to scare you guys. Thought I'd give it a try tonight." His mouth twitched with amusement as Winston chuckled along. Soon their laughter died away and the night was silent except for crickets chirping in the humid air.

Deion slapped Winston's shoulder. "I still think about Pam a lot, you know."

"Yeah, man, me, too." They settled on the steps of the side entrance near the garage. Winston sniffed. "Hey, do I smell chocolate?"

Deion lifted a white bakery box from the ground. "That cruise was my birthday gift to you. But I figured no birthday was complete without your favorite cake. Chocolate!" He jiggled the box in Winston's face.

"From Marcel's Bakery, with butter-cream frosting?"

"Of course. Nothing but the best for this day of the year."

Winston retrieved his keys and unlocked the door,

flipping the lights as they entered the kitchen. "You want coffee or milk with your cake?"

"You know me. I'm a milk man."

Winston removed the carton of milk and poured two glasses. He opened the box and inhaled. "Ahh. I haven't had one of these in ages." The white icing was decorated with bright green piping reading Happy Birthday Winston. He removed the cake and placed it on a china plate. After pulling a knife from the drawer, he cut two large pieces. "Oh, this is great." He closed his eyes, enjoying the sweet treat. They ate two pieces each before Winston placed the cake back in the box.

Deion noticed a picture on the counter. "Wow! Looks like you had a great time on that cruise. Who's the lovely lady?" He whistled as he gazed at Winston's favorite cruise photo, the one he told Rainy he'd always keep.

Winston pulled the picture away, the evening's events crashing back into his mind. Why were Jordan and Rainy arguing earlier? Did Jordan want her back?

"Hey, you look like you just saw a ghost. Don't tell me your cruise ship romance went sour already? What's the problem? Does she live far away? Take my advice, man, those long-distance romances never work." Winston tuned his brother out as he continued to spout words of advice about relationships.

"Hey." Deion snapped his fingers in front of his face. "Are you even listening to me anymore? What's up with the lady in the picture?"

"Oh, she lives here in Miami. But I don't know if we'll be seeing much of each other."

"Why?" Deion gazed at his brother, seemingly eager for more details.

"Oh, it's complicated. I thought things were fine until a few minutes ago."

Deion sat and scooted his chair toward Winston. "What happened a few minutes ago? Did you see this woman after the cruise docked? I got the idea to scare you after I sat here and waited for you for over an hour. I was wondering where you were."

"You're easily the nosiest man I've ever known. I'll tell you all about Rainy another time. Right now I'm tired, and I want to go to bed. Even eating two pieces of cake and milk isn't going to help me stay awake tonight."

Deion leaned back into the chair. "I'm not leaving until you give me some more details, brother. Like did you at least get some action?"

Winston glared at his brother. "What do you mean?"

"You know what I mean." He stood and leaned against the counter, gyrating his hips. "I'm talking about some sexual action. That way if you all stop speaking, at least you got something out of it."

Winston hung his head, gazing at the chocolate crumbs lining his plate. "I wish you would listen to what I've been telling you."

"Telling me? You're talking about that Christian stuff? Since Pam died, you've been a drag. I thought this cruise would snap you out of that funk."

Winston stood and looked his brother in the eye. "I'm serious about it. Since I've dedicated my life to

Christ, I'm doing my best not to go back to my old ways." He folded his arms. "I never lived the life of a saint, but you know for the most part that I've never been a promiscuous man. That's more your style."

"Yeah, I know, I know. But since you've been hurting and all, I figured you might meet a young lady on the cruise who'd help you forget your problems."

He placed his hand on Deion's shoulder. "I did. But having a good time with a woman doesn't always involve sleeping with her. You go to church sometimes. Don't you ever listen to the preacher?"

"Yeah, but you know how church folks are. They listen on Sunday, but do what they want the rest of the week."

"I used to be that way, but not anymore. I was active in the church after college, but I didn't openly admit my vow to Christ until after Pam's death."

"Does this woman you met share your beliefs?" Deion picked up Rainy's picture as he awaited Winston's response.

"Yeah. I told her that I was a Christian, but I didn't tell her that I was just baptized six months ago."

He shrugged his broad shoulders. "Why not? What difference does it make?"

"It shouldn't make a difference, but sometimes people who have been Christians a long time question the stability of new Christians. I've seen it happen. She knows about my problem with alcohol, and I don't want her to think I'm not strong enough in my faith to resist the urge to drink."

Deion shrugged again. "I don't get it. Why should you even care what she thinks? You don't even know if you'll be seeing her again. You just said so."

"That's enough about Rainy. It's time for you to leave. I'm tired."

"I can take a hint." He returned the picture to the counter before pulling Winston into a hug. "You had a good time on the cruise, though, right?"

Winston nodded as Deion released him. "And…are you sure you're okay with everything else?" Deion's hazel eyes were full of warmth and compassion as he gazed at his brother.

"Yeah, man, I'm fine. Now get out of here so I can get some sleep." He pushed his brother out the door.

He donned his ripped T-shirt and hole-filled shorts before dropping into bed. *Lord, please give me some guidance about my relationship with Rainy. If she's the right woman for me, I'm sure You'll do everything in Your power to make this work. Amen.* As he slumbered, his dreams were filled with images of Rainy and their glorious vacation cruise.

Rainy arrived at work early the following day. The newspaper office scurried with activity as people hurried to their desks while writers bustled about, trying to find the latest breaking story. She entered the accounting section of the building. Gray cubicles housed staff accountants as they added figures on calculators and entered journal entries into computers. She stopped to speak with a few of the workers before she entered her office.

Her assistant, Linda, rushed into the office. "Rainy, I'm so sorry." She pressed her hands together, drawing attention to her red, talon-like nails. Rainy wondered how she managed to type. Linda had dyed her dark hair again. Her platinum-colored locks clashed with her cocoa-brown skin.

"Linda, didn't we already have a talk about the company's dress code?" She eyed her assistant's short dark dress. The hemline was way above her knee, and the bodice stretched taut across her full breasts. At times, she wondered if Linda was there to work or to entice men.

She tossed her briefcase on the desk. "Now what are you sorry about?"

"Well, this guy called here last week. I know you told me if anybody called you during your vacation, I should take a name and phone number. Well, I forgot to get this man's name, and I think I mentioned that you'd gone on a cruise and would be returning on Sunday." She stared at her boss, wringing her hands.

Rainy folded her arms and glared at her assistant. "Listen, you need to remember the instructions I give you. How else am I going to run a successful accounting department?" She sighed as she sat in her leather chair.

Now she understood how Jordan knew about her return date. Well, she knew Linda's mistake couldn't be used as an excuse for the terrible end to her evening the previous day. Jordan would have found her sooner or later.

"I know. But after I had the conversation, I remembered that I hadn't taken down his name and phone number." She frowned as she gazed at her boss.

Rainy rolled her eyes as she twirled her chair toward the wall. She really needed to pray about the relationship she had with her assistant. She hoped the rumors she'd heard weren't true. She questioned Linda's integrity.

A few months before Rainy was promoted to accounting manager, she'd heard through office gossip that Linda was having an affair with her former boss, the previous manager. She'd apparently made some kind of demands on him, and threatened to go to Human Resources about their affair. However, before she could make any accusations, he resigned.

Rainy felt blessed when her hard work was rewarded with this position. She felt God was looking out for her by providing another outlet for her to release the pain and anger from her breakup. She didn't know if the rumors about Linda were true; however, she felt that the Lord wanted her to help this troubled woman. Linda left her office and returned minutes later with her steno pad and gold pen, eager to give a rundown of office events during her absence.

After their short meeting was over, she gave Linda a bright yellow flyer.

"You know how much I want my staff to benefit from the business seminars at the center in Miami. Well, there's a basic course on office professionalism that I think you should take. I've already signed you up for it. It's for two days, and breakfast and lunch are provided. You'll be going there on Thursday and Friday instead of reporting to work." Rainy had caught Linda openly flirting with several men in the company. At times she would leave her desk and not return for long periods.

She wondered if Linda was in search of another office affair. She prayed for patience, a virtue she needed when dealing with her assistant. Linda barely glanced at the flyer before placing it into her notebook. "Am I supposed to dress casual at the seminar?" She smoothed imaginary wrinkles from her tight dress. Even though a lot of offices in Miami adopted a casual dress code, their office was still business attire.

"No, it's business dress code for the seminar." Pausing, she gazed at her assistant. "And, please listen and try to learn something from the seminar. I think you might find some useful things to apply to your job."

Linda rolled her eyes and scratched her scalp. "Okay, whatever you say." She slammed her notebook shut. "You're having a lunch meeting later this week with three other managers. Did you want me to order food from the deli downstairs?"

Rainy nodded and told her what needed to be ordered. She gave her a box of Jamaican candy. "Put this out in the reception area so people can enjoy it."

"How was your trip?"

She managed to smile. "It went pretty well. I had a pleasant time." She had not gotten the pictures developed, but she assured her she would show them to the staff when they were ready.

After her assistant took her exit, Rainy gazed at her flooded inbox. She changed the message on her voice mail. She then lifted the stack of papers from her inbox and sorted through them.

Hours later, her growling stomach reminded her about lunch. As she left the air-conditioned building to go to her weekly lunch date with Sarah and Rachel, the Florida summer heat tinged her skin. She welcomed the cool air as she entered the restaurant.

"Hi, Ms. Jackson." The host approached bearing three menus. "I suppose your friends will be joining you?" She nodded as he led her to their regular table. Voices filled the room, and she had to strain to hear him. As she sat, he snapped her napkin open and placed it on her lap. "Enjoy your meal, Ms. Jackson, and I'll make sure to escort your friends over when they arrive." Before she could open her menu, Rachel and Sarah strutted into the restaurant. Both women looked like total opposites as they made their way to the table. Sarah's tall, dark frame contrasted with Rachel's short, chunky physique.

Sarah pulled Rainy into her arms. "Girl, you look good!" She sat and scanned the diners. Rainy rolled her eyes, leaning back into her chair. Sarah's manhunt was still in full swing. Her short hair glistened, and her gold hoop earrings swung as she gazed at the crowd. One reason they chose this restaurant as their regular lunch place was because it was known for having successful African-American clientele.

Rachel hugged Rainy, giving her an anxious smile. "You're as dark as wood, girl! You must have been in that sun a long time."

After they were served and said grace, Rachel searched through her purse. "Do you all mind if I pay for lunch on my credit card and you guys just give me the cash for your meal?"

Sarah glared at Rachel. "Good grief. You're always doing this. Can't you get your finances straight? You only want the money because you don't have any cash until payday." She ripped a roll apart and buttered it. "Besides, will your credit card even work? Seems like the last time we tried this, your card was declined, and me and Rainy had to pay for your meal."

Rachel's nut-brown skin reddened as she sipped from her water glass. "You're making a big deal out of nothing. Besides, I called my credit card company yesterday, and they gave me a three-hundred-dollar increase, so I should be set for lunch. I'll stop by the bank this afternoon to get a cash advance to pay you guys back for the last few lunches."

Sarah gritted her teeth. "Oh, you really need to make some changes in your life! You're never going get out of debt if you keep this up."

Rainy sighed as Rachel changed the topic. "Let's not talk about this now. How was the trip?"

Sarah's brown eyes widened with anticipation. She abandoned her roll and placed her hands on her hips as she gazed at Rainy. "Why didn't you call us when you stopped at your ports of call like you promised?"

Rainy stopped eating as she vaguely recalled the promise she made when they left her at the Port of Miami, and again on the phone that first night. "Well, I had a lot on my mind the past week." Her heart fluttered as she talked about the exotic places the cruise ship docked. Her friends listened intently to every word.

Sarah gave her a shrewd look as she polished off her burger and fries. "I know there's something you're not telling us."

Rachel was silent as she continued to eat her tuna salad. Their waiter returned and the tinkling of water and ice broke the silent moment.

Frowning, Rainy focused on the drops of moisture clinging to her water glass. She wanted to keep the knowledge of her new love interest to herself, for a little while anyway. However, she couldn't hide her happiness from her friends. Besides, since they were the ones who urged her to go on the cruise, they deserved to be the first to know. She took a deep breath and blurted, "I've met someone."

They stopped eating, staring. Rachel dropped her fork against the plate. "You're kidding."

Sarah folded her arms and pursed her lips. "Maybe I need to book myself on one of those cruises."

Rachel's large brown eyes glowed. "So what's he like?"

A hint of a smile touched Sarah's full lips. "What does he look like?"

Rachel placed her hands on her hips. "There's more to a man than the way he looks!"

Sarah chuckled, pushing her empty plate aside. She signaled the waiter to refill her soda. "Yeah, but if he looks good, there ain't nothing wrong with that!" Her gold hoop earrings swung as she laughed.

Rachel sighed and turned toward Rainy. "Is he a Christian?"

Questions continued to pop from one to the other. "Slow down. I can only answer one question at a time." She paused. "His name is Winston," she began. She told them about the man who'd made her happy during her voyage to the Caribbean islands. Of course, she didn't tell them everything, but she did stress that he lived in Miami and that he shared her Christian beliefs. "Oh, and did I mention that he's truly gorgeous?"

Rachel glowed as she listened to Rainy's story. "Well, if anybody deserves to meet a good Christian man, it's you. Especially after that stuff you went through with Jordan. You need to praise God that he's out of your life."

Rainy frowned as she pushed her plate of spaghetti and meatballs away. "I saw Jordan last night."

Rachel's eyes widened with surprise. "What do you mean you saw him last night? He's in London, right?"

She shook her head as she toyed with the white napkin in her lap. "No, his job assignment overseas is over so he's back in town, and from what I can gather, he's here to stay." She told them about her encounter with Jordan at church the previous evening.

Rachel gasped. "Winston was with you?"

She nodded. "Yes, he was, and he sure was mad."

Sarah crossed her legs. "That just shows how much Winston cares about you. So, Jordan really wants the two of you to get back together? What happened to his girlfriend in London?"

She squeezed her eyes shut, recalling the stormy night when Jordan called, delivering his painful message. She finally opened her eyes as Sarah placed her hand on her arm. "Hey, you okay? I didn't mean to bring up bad memories."

Rainy shook her head. "It's okay. I need to get over Jordan's deception sooner or later." She lifted her glass and took a drink of cold water. "I asked him about his British girlfriend, but he didn't answer me. I wouldn't be surprised if he got dumped and now he's crawling back to me, his ex-fiancée." She gazed at the patrons enshrouded in warm sunlight. "I hope he doesn't make a habit of approaching me. Now that he's back in town, I just hope that he leaves me alone."

She signaled the waiter for the check. It was time to get back to the office.

Chapter Seven

Rainy leaned back into her leather chair. She raised and lowered her shoulders several times, relieving the tension settling in her bones. She closed her eyes and tried to relax.

Linda knocked on her office door. "I'm leaving now. Did you need anything?" Rainy glanced at the clock. It was five o'clock, and she knew her assistant wasn't crazy about overtime.

"No, I'm fine." She waved her away.

A few hours later she glanced at the clock again. *It's seven-thirty.* Weariness consumed her as she slowly stood.

After a hot soak in a bubble bath, perhaps she would feel better. She was starving. She already missed the elaborate meals they served on the cruise. How she wished for one of the thick juicy steaks they served for dinner! She said goodbye to the remaining co-workers before she exited the building. The bright sun spilled on the crowded sidewalk. She removed her shades from her purse and placed them over her eyes.

As she walked to the adjoining garage, she thought about the baked fish and salad she was having for dinner. She needed to resume her healthy eating habits. She also wanted to call Winston. She hoped he didn't feel slighted when she'd spoken to Jordan the previous night.

"Rainy!" She glanced across the street and stiffened. Jordan walked toward her, wearing a custom-made suit and carrying a leather briefcase. *Was he waiting for me?* She stood in the same spot, frozen. Cars honked as he finished crossing the street. He had not waited for the walk signal.

Drops of moisture clung to his forehead as a tentative smile tipped the corners of his lips. "I've been waiting across that street in this heat for over an hour! You need to learn to leave your job on time and not work too hard."

Nostalgic memories flooded her mind as she sniffed his familiar aftershave. He touched her arm and she stepped away.

"What do you want?" Her voice was a whisper amid the busy traffic.

A group of sun-bleached, tanned teenagers ran across the street in their beach attire. One of them collided into Jordan. "Yo, sorry, dude!" He hurried to rejoin his friends. Jordan glared at the boy as he brushed granules of sand from his suit.

"Those kids need to stop running around like a pack of animals!" His dark eyes glared with malice.

She watched the group disappear down the street. "You get so upset over the smallest things."

He cleared his throat. "Who cares about those stupid kids? Besides, I wanted to continue the conversation we started last night. Since your new boyfriend isn't with you, I figured we could talk without interruptions."

Her glare was met with his continued smile. "Let me take you out to dinner. We can go to Raymond's." He knew Raymond's was her favorite restaurant. Her stomach growled, announcing her hunger. He chuckled. "I see some things never change. You still have the loudest stomach." He tousled her hair and attempted a clumsy embrace.

She swallowed as she backed into a nearby building. What should she do? If he wanted to speak with her, he would just keep showing up at inopportune times until she agreed to listen. If she had dinner with him this evening, maybe he would leave her alone. Perhaps she could convince him that attending her church would not be in his best interests since that scheme would fail to win her back.

"Okay, I'll have dinner with you." He beamed like a child on Christmas morning. "But just this once. We're not making this a habit." She pressed her hands together so hard, they ached. She silently prayed for guidance in this sticky situation.

Since Raymond's was a few blocks away, they opted to walk. The warm Florida breeze blew over her hot skin. Tiny beads of perspiration ran down her back as they entered the restaurant. The cool, dim interior provided welcome relief. Jazz music played over the speakers and minutes later the server showed them to their table. "Enjoy your meal." She gave them plastic-laminated menus.

"Before we order, I think you owe me an explanation. Why do you want to resume our relationship?"

He took her hand and stroked her fingers. She slapped his hand away and threw her menu on the table. "Don't you dare touch me, Jordan! If you keep this behavior up, I'm not having dinner with you." She tried hard to keep her temper in check as she stood. He frowned as if he'd lost his most prized possession.

"Baby, don't leave. I promise I'll behave myself." He hung his head in shame as he toyed with a napkin.

She sighed as she sat back down on the cushioned chair. "I just don't understand you. You break our engagement and suddenly you want me to welcome you back with open arms? Why?"

"I want you back because I love you." He reached toward her but pulled away, as he seemingly recalled her recent outburst.

She gritted her teeth, taking a deep breath. "That's lame. You said you loved me before you went to London, but that didn't stop you from finding someone else. You never did tell me what happened to your London girlfriend anyway." She folded her arms, wondering if she was a fool to spend time with him. She closed her eyes and again prayed for guidance. Jordan's reentrance into her life was causing so much pain and bitterness to erupt within her, like a steaming volcano ready to explode. She needed to work on tempering these feelings. Should she witness to him, try to convince him to give Christianity a chance? She didn't think she could utter those words.

His fingers brushed her arm. "Are you okay, baby?"

She opened her eyes and threw her napkin on the table. Her chair grated against the wooden floor as she stood once again. "I don't think dinner is a good idea after all." She turned and left the restaurant.

Winston entered Raymond's restaurant with a few of his co-workers. They insisted on taking him out to dinner for his birthday. He stopped as they were shown to their table. He spotted Rainy with her no-good ex-boyfriend. He watched her slap his arm. He was about to go to her table to see if she needed help, but her anger abated and she returned to her seat.

He sighed as he walked to the table that his co-workers had reserved. He could no longer see Rainy and her dinner partner from the table. He glanced at his menu. His co-workers urged him to order the most expensive entrée. However, he had lost his appetite. Rainy Jackson filled a secret place in his heart, and now he wondered if that place was about to become empty again.

Thoughts of her aborted dinner appointment with Jordan still filled Rainy's mind the following day as she sat at a lunch table in the company cafeteria. As she ate her tuna salad sandwich, she attempted to lull the other managers into conversation, eager to try to forget about Jordan's sudden interest. She told them about her cruise ship vacation, showing pictures she'd recently had developed at the one-hour photo store.

After lunch, she strolled into her office and immediately noticed the fresh scent of lilies swirling through the room. The white elongated leaves tickled her nose as she touched her face to the budding blossoms.

Linda peeked into the office, clutching a small cream-colored envelope. "The card fell out when the delivery man left the flowers."

Rainy plucked the card from Linda's outstretched hand. She hovered in the doorway. "Is there anything else?"

She brushed her hands over her platinum locks. "Uh, I guess that's it for now."

After Rainy closed her door, she slit the sealed envelope with a letter opener. *I hope these flowers are from Winston and not Jordan.* She scanned the letter and read the following words:

Dear Rainy,
Please meet me at the park today at 5:30.
Your friend,
Winston.

She sighed, running her fingers over the thick paper. As she settled into her chair, her phone rang. She lifted the receiver. "Rainy Jackson speaking."

"Rainy Jackson, this is Winston Michaels." His deep voice sounded stilted and formal. "Did you get my flowers, sweetheart?"

She caressed one of the buds. "Yes, I got them." She sighed as she continued to stare at the flowers. "Thank you, they're lovely. Why do you want to meet in the park today?"

"I'll explain that when we meet this evening. That is, if we *are* meeting." His deep voice hardened, and she gripped the phone.

"I have some errands to run tonight but I can meet you. You sound so…so upset. Is something wrong? Frankly, I'm confused. You send me flowers and ask me to meet you, but your tone indicates to me that you're angry." She paused and chewed on her lower lip. "Besides, you want to meet me right after work. I won't even have time to go home and change."

"Don't change. I like seeing you in a dress."

"How do you even know I'm wearing a dress today?"

"I just figured you wore suits and dresses to work all the time. Besides, I've got a nice surprise for you. Just come to the park after work…please?" He sounded like a child begging for the last cookie in the jar.

"Oh, okay. I'll meet you in the park. But which one?"

He told her which park she needed to go to. "And you promise you won't go home and change?"

"I promise."

After work she took the expressway to the park. She

pulled into the deserted parking lot and turned her engine off. She wiggled her toes in her flat shoes as she stared through her sunroof. Birds flew in the clear blue sky, their twittering song carrying over the summer breeze. Clouds, as white and fluffy as cotton balls, nestled in the heavens. She closed her eyes and enjoyed the light summer breeze. She thought about the exquisite lilies, still sitting on her desk at work.

She finally got out of her car and stretched before she walked through the wooded path into the adjoining picnic section. Squirrels scattered around the trees as they hunted for food. The palm leaves fluttered in the wind as she made her way toward Winston. She'd spotted him right away in the small picnic area. He sat under a large oak tree. A roaring fire burned from the flaming barbeque grill. His hazel eyes softened as he spotted her walking through the trees.

"I'm glad you made it here." He spread a blanket over the seat of the picnic table. "I don't want you to get that pretty dress dirty." He gestured toward the blanket.

She sat as she smoothed wrinkles from her navy-blue dress. A nautical pattern decorated the sleeves and the buttons, and it was her favorite.

He cleared his throat as he opened a package of hot dogs. "Our meal is going to be short and simple since I know you've got some things to do tonight."

She settled on the wooden bench as birds swooped to the ground, eagerly seeking stray crumbs. She watched the corded muscles in his arms as he turned the hot dogs over the coals. The scent of freshly grilled meat filled the air as he took a paper plate and removed their food.

He set the plate in the middle of the table and opened a cooler and removed two ice-cold sodas. He popped the tops and gave her one of the frosty cans. Drops of moisture clung to her fingers as she lifted the refreshing drink to her lips. He suddenly clamped her wrist in a firm squeeze. "Don't drink that yet."

She looked into his hazel eyes. Her soda was still raised in her arm, and warmth traveled through her wrist from his touch. "Why not?"

He sighed as he released her wrist and raised his can of soda. "Because. Before you take the first drink, I'd like to propose a toast." He lifted his can into the air. "To us."

She raised her soda. "To us." Her voice was barely audible in the secluded park. She sipped her drink while he fixed her hot dog, just as she liked it. "You know I'm dying to know why you suddenly wanted to go on this picnic. Why did you send me those lilies?"

He placed her hot dog on a plate and poured potato chips from a cellophane bag alongside it. He placed her meal in front of her. "You don't like the flowers?"

She nibbled on a chip. "I love the flowers. But I sense you have a reason for suddenly doing all of this." She gestured toward the simple impromptu meal.

The wooden bench creaked as he sat beside her. He pulled her hand into his and kissed each of her fingertips. "I know we've only known each other for about a week and a half, but I can honestly say that it's been one of the happiest times of my life." He cleared his throat as he continued to caress her hand. "But, you've got to be straight with me. I need to know where I stand."

Her stomach felt as if it was full of fluttering butterflies. She sighed as she gazed into his gorgeous hazel eyes. "What do you mean?"

His Adam's apple bobbed as he swallowed. "My coworkers took me out to dinner last night. I saw you at Raymond's restaurant with Jordan." She cringed as she looked away. "I know you were pretty upset on the cruise about your breakup with your boyfriend. Now I know he's back in the picture. Are you thinking about giving your relationship with him another chance? If that's the case, then I need to know right now. Do you still have feelings for Jordan? What's going on?"

She pushed her plate aside as her appetite diminished. "I didn't have a date planned with Jordan last night." She explained how he'd cornered her after she left her job.

He rubbed her back and warm currents of pleasure flowed through her. "Is this dude stalking you? Maybe you should call the police. Or I can talk to him and make sure he stops bothering you."

She sighed as he continued to massage her back. "I went to dinner with Jordan willingly. He didn't force me to go with him. If you'd watched us long enough, you would have seen that I got upset and left the restaurant before we even ordered dinner."

"That's a relief. Is he going to leave you alone now?"

She huffed. "I doubt it. He's very competitive. Plus, I wonder if the Lord is placing him in my path for a reason. Maybe if Jordan attends my church enough, just to pursue me, some of the messages from the sermons might make him accept Christ."

He shrugged. "I don't know about that. I don't know all the details about your breakup with him, but I do sense that he's up to no good right now, and you should watch your back." He continued to run his fingers over her spine. "Or, if it'll make you feel better, I'll watch it for you."

She swallowed as her temperature rose. She tried to calm her racing heart. *Being around Winston seems to have a big physical effect on me!* She moved away from his eager hand as she toyed with the chips on her plate. "I never told you all the details about the breakup because it was too painful to talk about."

"I'm your friend. You can talk to me about anything."

She then told him about her engagement to Jordan and about the thunderous night when he broke their engagement. "I'm still working on releasing my anger toward him. I hated being dumped. It's one of the worse feelings I'd ever experienced. Nobody wants to be told that they're not loved anymore." She pushed her fingers through her hair and rested her forehead in her palm. "It's even worse when you're being dumped for another woman. I felt cheated and used. I felt so many negative things that night. But my faith in God helped me through that rough time, and I'm still leaning on Him, hoping to dispense all these negative feelings toward Jordan."

"Oh, sweetheart. You never told me you two were engaged and he cheated on you. That must have been pretty rough."

"It was. I never saw it coming. I gave him my whole heart and I trusted him completely." She watched the smoke curl from the extinguished barbeque flame.

He pulled the napkin she'd unconsciously been shredding from her fingers and massaged her hand. "So, do you still love Jordan? Are you even thinking about taking him back?"

She shook her head. "I can't take him back. I wish him the best, but I don't think I could ever trust him again. It's time for me to move on and forget about him."

He sighed as he released her hand and fixed himself a plate of food. "Well, this picnic is now an official celebration. Hopefully, in due time, you'll learn to trust *me*."

After he set his plate on the table, she pulled him into an embrace, inhaling the scent of his cologne.

"You already have a great deal of my trust. You give me a good feeling, and I'm touched that you sent me the lilies and fixed me this meal." He pressed his lips to hers and they shared a kiss. Her knees felt like jelly as she pulled her plate toward her. Her stomach growled loudly. "I think my appetite has returned," she said with a laugh.

"Oh, before you eat, I wanted to ask you something."

"What?"

He nervously cleared his throat. "Well, I like you, so I think we should start spending some time together regularly and see what happens between us."

She grinned. "Winston, that's a wonderful idea."

He said grace before they enjoyed their celebration meal.

Chapter Eight

Winston whistled as he unlocked the door and entered his house. As he removed his running shoes, grains of sand spilled onto his dark carpet. He threw the shoes in the corner and lay on the couch.

He was still fatigued from his vigorous run on South Beach. The crowds, traffic and artsy buildings did little to take his mind off of Rainy.

It had been two months since he'd arranged the special picnic for her at the park. They'd been out several times, and he found himself growing closer to her as the days rolled by. For the Fourth of July, he'd taken her to the beach to view the fireworks. Just being with her made the bright colors in the midnight sky look more enticing. The thought of touching liquor never crossed his mind when he was with her.

When the oblivion of sleep almost enveloped him into its depths, he forced himself to get into the shower.

Thirty minutes later, he snuggled beneath his clean cotton sheets. He closed his eyes and prayed that the Lord would make their relationship work.

The piercing ring of the phone awakened his deep slumber. His eyes fluttered open, and he gazed at the red digital display of his clock. *It's three a.m.* He grabbed the phone. "Hello?"

"Winston? It's Aunt Gladys." He clutched the phone tightly as her pain and hysteria carried over the wire.

"Aunt Gladys?" He blinked as his foggy brain cleared. He sat up and threw his feet to the floor, his sheets and blankets cascading to the edge of the bed. "What's wrong?"

"Can you come by?" Masculine yells and screams filled the background.

"Is that Uncle Greg?"

"Yes, please come by—hurry," she pleaded before hanging up. He rolled out of bed and dressed in a tattered T-shirt and jeans. Fifteen minutes later, he knocked on his aunt's door. The night was warm and humid, and sweat trickled down his face as he watched a lizard race across the steps. The small porch was illuminated with a warm glow as the light came on. His aunt opened the door, wearing her blue bathrobe. Her gray hair was in curlers and she had circles under her eyes.

"Oh, thanks for coming. Greg just found out he's lost his job! Since he's in his fifties, he doesn't know if he'll find another one. He was out half the night and he came home drunk. You were the first person I called." Tears streamed from her dark eyes as she clutched his hand and led him into the living room. The house looked like it had been sitting in the middle of a cyclone. Books and papers were strewn everywhere. Broken china figurines littered the floor. "He finally calmed down just before you got here. You know how alcohol affects him."

He sighed as he followed her into the bedroom. His uncle lay on the bed, his loud snores filling the room.

Gladys pulled him into the kitchen. "I'm making some coffee. I'm so glad you came. You're the only one who understands Greg."

He sat at the chipped wooden table. Memories of holidays and Sunday dinners flooded his mind as he gazed around the familiar kitchen. "Did you call my dad?"

She sighed. "No, but I thought about it. Out of all his brothers, Greg is closest to your father." She paused, leaning against the wall. "But you know, I just had a feeling that I should call you. Since you and Greg have been through similar experiences, I figured you'd understand. Besides, now that your parents have moved, your father wouldn't have been able to come by tonight and I knew you would be able to come."

He gazed at the bright yellow paper decorating the walls and the large bowl of fruit resting on the table. A pound cake sat on the counter in a glass case. She removed a knife from the oak drawer and removed the lid covering the cake. She cut several slices.

He toyed with the rose-decorated china cup. "You know, you're right. I do understand Uncle Greg a lot.

He was there for me when I wanted to get clean and sober. He also introduced me to the world of Alcoholics Anonymous."

He continued, "You know, I don't think I'd have been able to stick to my sobriety if it hadn't been for his support and my deep faith in God."

She poured the coffee, adding cream and sugar. She placed the cake on a platter and set it in the middle of the table. She served him a piece of the cake. "I know. My husband is a sweet man. I just wish he were strong enough to resist temptation. What am I going to do?"

Notes from the slow jazz station filled the kitchen with somber music as the old wooden clock steadily ticked the minutes away.

"Maybe he'll feel better tomorrow. There's no guarantee he'll be like this every night."

She nodded. "I know. I was so disappointed when he came home that way. I was worried when he didn't come home after work. But then he came in drunk and upset. While he was tearing up stuff in the house, he yelled about his layoff from the job." She paused and sipped her coffee. A commercial about a local restaurant played on the radio. An orange tabby cat trotted into the kitchen and jumped onto her lap, falling almost instantly asleep. "Can you call him and spend some time with him over the next few days? Maybe you can convince him that this is a mistake."

"When he wakes up and sees the damage he's done to this house, he might be convinced."

She sighed and rubbed her temple. She caressed the

cat's fur, and scratched his ears. "I hope he can find a decent job. You know how unsteady the economy has been lately."

"Yeah, I know. I'll check around at the bank. They might have something there. He might also want to look into contacting a headhunter. Sometimes companies might want an older person on board, knowing how much experience they can bring to the company." They sat in comfortable silence, the gentle purring of the cat mingling with the music on the radio.

"Well, have you been okay? I know Deion gave you that cruise as a birthday gift a few months ago. I've been meaning to call you since I know it was your first birthday alone." She touched his hand and he smiled for the first time that evening.

"Thanks. I've been okay. I met a wonderful woman on the cruise."

"Really?" She beamed. "So, tell me, do you think she's the one?"

He sighed. "I don't know. I like her a lot. But there's so much to consider."

"Such as?" She released his hand, refilled their coffee cups and served him another slice of cake.

"Well, for starters, she's still hurting from a broken relationship. She says she wants to forget her ex-fiancé, but I think he's still on her mind."

"Well, most women have had relationships before they meet the right man."

"But this is different." He told her about Rainy's situation.

"So, her ex-fiancé wants to patch things up with her?"

He nodded. "He came back to town right after we came back from the cruise. He hasn't approached her lately, but he does show up at her church sometimes."

"Just pray about it, that's all you can do. If it was meant to be, then it'll happen."

He placed his chin in his hand as he continued to think about Rainy. "That's not the only reason I'm worried."

"Well, what else could be wrong? You're not involved with anybody else right now, are you?"

He shook his head. "No, it's nothing like that."

"Well, what is it then?" she prompted.

He sighed as he stared at the sleeping cat. "I'm not getting any younger. If I get married, I want to make sure it's forever, and I'd want to have children."

"Of course you would. That's the way God made us. You're thirty-five and it's time you settled down and had a family."

"Well, after seeing Uncle Greg tonight, I don't know if I can do that."

"What does Greg have to do with your getting married?" She looked puzzled as she placed the sleeping cat on the floor. She then washed their dirty coffee cups and placed them in the dish rack.

"Well, you know how I used to have a drinking problem."

"Yes?" She wiped her hands on a dish towel and rejoined him at the table.

"Well, what if something bad happens and I started drinking again?" He gazed at the messy living room to emphasize his point. "I can't expose my wife and children to this kind of behavior. It's scary what alcohol can do to a person."

"You know me and Greg were never blessed with children, but you listen to me. You're too levelheaded to allow this to happen to your family. I love Greg, but sometimes he can be so…impulsive. You're not like that. I'm sure that your first birthday without Pam has been hard on you, and I'm sure you didn't go out and drink yourself into oblivion."

"I didn't. But I'm not going to say the thought didn't cross my mind. It's hard to stay away from alcohol when you're hurting."

"I know, honey, I know." When she gave him a brief hug, he sniffed her familiar jasmine perfume. "But you're a strong Christian man. Since you gave up alcohol, you renewed your faith in the Lord, and that's all you're going to need to fight any of your ghosts from the past. I wish Greg had stopped and said a prayer when he lost his job, instead of running off to some bar." She slapped her hand against the table. "Don't let Greg's actions ruin any happiness you might find for yourself."

Soon, the birds' lilting cadence reminded him it was a new day. Warm fingers of sunlight brightened the kitchen. "I've got to leave to get ready for work." He kissed her cheek as he left her home.

Over the next few days, Winston spent a lot of time with his uncle Greg. He took him out to dinner and they had a long talk. They attended midweek church service, and they asked the reverend to say a special prayer for Greg's job hunt. His uncle admitted to the depressed feeling he had when he discovered his unemployed status. "I just went to the bar, Winston. I'm sorry. I know it was wrong, but I did it anyway. I was just feeling so bad."

He was relieved Uncle Greg stayed sober for the next few days. He had a plan to follow—trying to find a job. "Who wants to hire a fifty-year-old man?" Greg grumbled.

"Don't be so discouraged, Uncle Greg. You've barely started looking for a job. Give it some time." He hoped and prayed his uncle followed his advice.

Winston thought about his uncle as he trudged to his car after work a few weeks later, throwing his briefcase in the back seat. The shaded parking garage barely deflected the Florida summer heat. He blasted his air conditioner as he drove to the parking attendant's station. The attendant's Jamaican accent echoed in the wide lot. "Have a nice weekend, Winston. Can't believe you stayed this late on a Friday."

Grunting a response, Winston took his exit. As he drove home, he listened to the DJ on the radio spouting words of joy about the upcoming weekend. Tourists cluttered the streets, searching for the perfect way to spend their vacation. A dull ache clutched his gut when he drove past Rainy's workplace. He still had not attempted to call or visit her since he'd witnessed his uncle in a drunken stupor.

An hour later, he had changed into his old comfortable clothes and lay on the couch. He turned his TV on and flipped through the channels. Soon, he abandoned the remote and closed his eyes. Dreams of the kisses he'd shared with Rainy cluttered his mind. He tossed on the narrow couch as his heart continued to pound. *Bang!* He fell to the floor, bumping his arm against the coffee table. He clamped his mouth shut as he awakened.

As he rubbed his arm, a soft tapping noise filtered through the living room. He sluggishly stood on his wobbly legs. He glanced at the clock and noticed it was almost 9:00 p.m. It took him a moment to realize the sound was coming from the front door. He shuffled to the entrance. "Deion, I'm tired and not in the mood for visitors." He yanked the door open.

"Rainy." He clutched the door handle. She was wearing an enticing tangerine-colored dress, and her hair hung loosely around her shoulders. He longed to sift the tresses through his fingers. He lifted his hand toward her, but lowered it abruptly, quickly stepping away.

He swallowed, trying to relieve his dry throat. "What are you doing here?"

"Are you expecting your brother?"

"How did you know where I lived?" He wanted to resist temptation while they were dating. So he always picked her up at her place and they frequented public places without coming to his house or hers.

"We exchanged addresses on the cruise, remember?"

Of course he remembered. Her address would be emblazoned in his mind forever. "Come in." He touched her arm as she entered his home. She gazed around his darkened living room, surveying her surroundings. He looked around his house, wondering how it would look through the eyes of a newcomer.

Newspapers were scattered on his floor. His scarred coffee table was decorated with dried rings of wetness from his drinking glasses. His living room furniture was old, but comfortable. A large color TV dominated the room. An old poinsettia plant was in the corner, dead.

"You have a nice home."

"You think so?"

She nodded. "It looks so comfortable." She gazed at his worn couch.

"You're welcome to sit down."

She sat and crossed her long legs. He touched her arm again and relished the softness of her skin.

"So, is Deion supposed to be coming by?" He gazed into the depths of her liquid brown eyes.

"Um, no, I'm not expecting Deion. I just assumed you were him since he's the only person that drops by uninvited." He swallowed as sweat trickled down his forehead.

"You look tired. Did I wake you up?" She frowned as she continued to look at him. "What's wrong?"

"Nothing. Why do you ask?"

She shrugged as she toyed with a tassel on his pillow. "You just seem upset." They were quiet for several seconds.

"Are you hungry?" His voice broke the thick silence engulfing the room. Before she could answer, her stomach growled, loud.

They laughed, breaking the tense moment. "I guess that's a yes. Did you want to order a pizza?"

She nodded. They decided on an extra-large pizza with extra cheese, pepperoni and mushrooms. She touched his arm as he replaced the phone into the cradle after ordering the pizza. "I really wanted to talk to you."

Winston's stomach growled. "I want to talk to you, too. How about we do that after we've eaten?"

She chewed her lower lip and gazed at the TV. An old *Good Times* rerun played, and J.J. strutted onto the screen wearing bright red pajamas. She smiled, showing her perfect white teeth.

She nodded. "Okay."

Minutes later, they entered the kitchen. "You know, I usually eat my dinner in the living room, in front of the TV. But since you're my dinner guest, I'll set the table."

As he placed the dishes on the table, she chopped vegetables for a salad. He fixed a pitcher of iced tea with lemons. His hunger for food consumed him, however, his need to be with Rainy, talking, laughing, was stronger than his craving for nourishment. Her back was turned toward him, and he was about to enfold her trim body in his arms when the doorbell rang, announcing the arrival of the pizza deliveryman.

He returned to the kitchen moments later and placed

the pie in the middle of the table. They sat and he pulled her slim brown hands into his. After he'd prayed over the simple meal, visions of their shared elaborate cruise dinners flashed through his mind. He pushed the memories aside as they enjoyed the pizza.

"I'm so stuffed that I don't think I could eat another bite," she announced, placing her hand over her flat stomach. He poured more glasses of iced tea and carried them into the living room. An old rerun of *The Jeffersons* was playing on TV.

She settled on the couch. "I feel so much better since I've eaten. I know you're probably wondering why I'm here. I wanted to ask you a favor."

He raised his eyebrows, surprised. "A favor?"

"Yes. You met a lot of people when you went to church with me."

He nodded. "It's a nice congregation. Everybody is so friendly and it's small. Large churches are nice, but I like the family feeling you get from a small church."

"Well, do you remember our conversation on the cruise?"

"We had several conversations on the cruise."

"I'm talking about the conversation we had in the photo shop. Remember I told you about the youth financial seminars at Friendship Community Church? You offered to help me and I'd like to take you up on your offer." She removed papers from her briefcase.

"But?"

She sighed. "I just wasn't sure…"

"You mean you weren't sure if I still wanted to help

you? When I make a promise, I try my best to keep it. I'm a man of my word, and I know the Lord doesn't condone lying."

She dropped the papers, stood, and paced his carpeted floor. He muted the television. "You're not being honest with me. What happened?" She gave him a frank, unwavering gaze as she returned to the couch. Before he could answer, she continued. "You don't know how much I agonized and prayed about coming over here today."

"I can imagine you would pray about coming over here. You're a spiritual woman, and you have a deep faith in the Lord. That's one of the things I admire most about you." He raised his hand, almost touching her hair, but he quickly lowered it and turned away.

"Why can't you look at me? What's wrong with you? What's wrong with me? When I didn't hear from you over the past few weeks, I figured you were busy at your job or something. When you had that special picnic for me at the park and suggested we try to have a relationship, I thought you had a good idea." She folded her arms. "We had a good time on the cruise, and for the two months afterward." She gazed around his cluttered living room. "I was going to call tonight to see how you were. I don't know if you've realized this about me, but I'm a direct person. If I have a problem, I go straight to the source, if that's possible." A car parked on the street, the grating motor and honking horn disturbing the silent room. "I know it's forward of me to show up here, unannounced, but I wanted to know the truth, and I figured it was best if I came in person."

He nodded. "I can understand that."

"You remember I got scared on the cruise? I avoided you all day? Well, I was being childish, and I should've told you what was on my mind from the start. I'm telling you what's on my mind now."

He nodded. "I appreciate your honesty." He scooted closer to her and pried her hands apart. He took her hand and traced the faint lines in her palm. "I like you. While we were on the cruise, I thought we might begin seeing each other once we docked in Miami. We've had a wonderful two months together, but now I'm not so sure we should continue this relationship."

"Why?" He could barely hear her. He was so close to her that her light floral scent filled his nostrils. His heart was pounding for dear life, and he fought not to enfold this beautiful woman in his arms.

He looked at the television. George Jefferson was yelling at Tom Willis. He recalled Uncle Greg's drunken rage. He abandoned *The Jeffersons* and gazed at her again.

She stood. "I guess I'd better leave."

"No, don't leave. It's so complicated."

"Did I imagine the chemistry we shared over the past few months?" She toyed with the strap of her leather purse.

"No, you didn't imagine that." He took a deep breath.

She sat down again as she continued to look at him.

Her dark eyes were full of curiosity and he squirmed under her intense gaze. "You're hiding something from me."

"Rainy—"

She lifted her arm and pressed her palm toward his face in a stopping motion. "Don't deny it! I know we've only known each other for a couple of months, but I can tell when you've got something on your mind. The last time you acted like this, you told me later about how you were sad since Pam died. Has that still been bothering you?" He shook his head. "Well, what is it?" She threw her hands up in the air, exasperated. "You don't want to tell me?"

"No. It's something personal. I'm still struggling with it and I'm still praying about it. I'm sure if the time is right, I'll tell you."

She bit her lower lip while looking perplexed. Her shoulders slumped as she gathered her financial seminar papers. "Does this have to do with your alcoholism? Did you turn to drink again?" She clutched the papers so hard that they wrinkled.

He gazed at her, startled. He swallowed hard as words seemed to fail him. "Do you have so little faith in me? You're accusing me of drinking?" She shrank from his intense gaze as she dropped the papers in her briefcase.

"Maybe working together on this project is a bad idea. If I've upset you, then I'm sorry."

"Rainy, I don't know if this will work or not."

"You're talking about the youth seminars?"

He shook his head. "I'm not sure if our dating would work. But I did give you my word to work on the youth financial seminars at the church, so I will do that. You're my sister in Christ, and I think we should be friends for now, and see what happens after that."

She nodded. Her voice rang clear and strong as she outlined what the program entailed. They would work together for the next several Saturday mornings, educating the youth of Friendship Community Church about proper budgeting and financial skills.

She stood and gathered her purse and her briefcase. "I guess I'll be seeing you next Saturday morning for the seminar?"

He nodded. "I'll see you on Saturday." He watched her as she walked out of his house and to her car. He parted his curtains and watched her taillights disappear as she drove away.

Grabill Missionary Church Library
P.O. Box 279
13637 State Street
Grabill, IN 46741

Chapter Nine

Rainy threw her briefcase and purse on her couch. Hot tears spilled from her eyes as she recalled her conversation with Winston. She got on her knees and leaned her elbows on the couch cushions. She issued a prayer, asking for guidance in her situation with Winston.

When she stood on her shaky legs, her phone rang. She was tempted not to answer, but forced herself to lift the receiver. "Hello."

Sarah's strong voice carried over the wire. "Lorraine Jackson, where have you been? Don't you know it's after midnight?"

She gazed at her clock adorned with Roman numerals. It was 12:00 a.m. She plopped onto the couch and flipped the sandals off her feet. She wiggled her toes as she tried to relax. "You sound like you're chastising me."

"Have you lost your mind? You were supposed to be here at nine-thirty tonight! We were supposed to watch videos and eat popcorn, remember?"

Suddenly, she did remember. She was on her way to Sarah's when she stopped at Winston's. Once she saw him, all thought and logic had escaped her, and she abandoned her evening with Sarah. "I'm so sorry. I'll make it up to you, though. Come by for lunch tomorrow."

Sarah didn't respond for several seconds. Rainy closed her eyes and relished the silence. "You sound awful. What happened? I was about to call the police and hospitals. I was convinced you'd been in a car accident."

She sniffed and removed a tissue from the box on the coffee table. "I just need to sleep now. I don't have energy to talk. Can you come by tomorrow around noon? We'll talk then. We can fill Rachel in when she returns from visiting her sick grandmother on Sunday night."

"Okay, I'll say a quick prayer for you tonight."

"Thanks. I think I'll need one."

The next day she slept until eleven o'clock. By the time she showered and changed, she heard Sarah's hard knock on the door. When she opened it, Sarah greeted her with two large oily paper sacks. "You sounded terrible on the phone last night. So I figured you could use one of your favorite cheese steak sandwiches for lunch. I also brought fries and something special." She scurried into the house, dropped the bags in the kitchen and returned to her car. Seconds later, she entered carrying a white bakery box.

"I got your favorite white chocolate cheesecake from Marcel's Bakery. I was fortunate to get it. It was the last one they had! I figured God wanted me to buy this cheesecake to cheer up my best friend." Sarah's brown eyes twinkled as she grinned. After she delivered the box to the kitchen table, she embraced Rainy. "Now, when we eat our lunch, you'll need to tell me all about it."

Rainy opened a bag, and the strong smell of onions and fried meat filled the air. Her mouth watered and her stomach growled. After they sat at the table, Sarah said grace. As she tasted her sandwich, she noticed Sarah's immaculate attire. She sported a casual cranberry dress and leather sandals. "You were just coming over to see me for lunch. There was no need for you to get gussied up." She grinned before she bit into her sandwich.

Sarah popped a fry into her mouth and gulped her soda before responding. "I have some other things to do this afternoon."

She continued to gaze at her friend. "What things? I get the feeling there's a reason why you're dressed like that." She sniffed the air. "Plus you're wearing that expensive perfume! Who are you trying to impress?"

"Can't you take a hint? I don't want to talk about my plans for later."

"What plans? Did another guy answer your ad? Are you going to meet him this afternoon?"

Sarah sighed as she pushed her sandwich aside. "Well…yes, I'm going to meet a guy this afternoon."

Rainy dipped her fry in a puddle of ketchup. "Well,

what's the big secret? I want details!" She popped the
fry in her mouth and eagerly awaited Sarah's response.

"How many times do I have to tell you, I don't want
to talk about him?"

"Are you falling in love?"

"My goodness, no. This is the first time I'm meeting this guy." She sipped her soda.

"I'll let you off the hook this time, but you'll need
to fill me and Rachel in eventually. I can't stand secrets!"

After they finished their lunch, Rainy opened the bakery box. She enjoyed the buttery rich scent of the cheesecake as she cut two slices and placed them on small china
plates. She brewed coffee, and as they enjoyed the luscious dessert she told Sarah about her visit to Winston's
house. "I honestly didn't think I'd take that long to see
him. If I was thinking clearly, I would've called you."

After they were finished eating, Sarah voiced her
concerns. "So do you think you're falling in love with
Winston?"

"I can't help the way I feel. I've only been in love a
few times in my life, and each time it happens quickly."

Sarah shrugged as she poured another cup of fragrant coffee. Curls of steam floated in the air as she
grasped her mug. "Well, maybe you're not over Jordan
yet. When we left you on that cruise, you looked like a
little girl who was leaving her mother for the first time."

"So?" Rainy walked to the sink and rinsed her coffee cup. She placed it in the dishwasher before returning to the table.

"So? When it comes to relationships, you're clueless."

Her mouth dropped open. "You're one to speak, looking through Christian dating ads. They should call you 'desperately seeking Sarah.' I'm offended!"

Sarah squeezed Rainy's hand. "Look, I don't mean to offend you, but it's true. You jumped into that engagement with Jordan so quickly and you were still hurting over the breakup when we left you on the cruise ship." She paused, gazing at her red, manicured nails. "And now you're telling me that you met Winston, and that made the pain vanish?" She released her hand and leaned back into the chair.

Rainy turned away, ashamed she had fallen for Winston so easily and in such a short time. She was also ashamed for the way she had been treated by Jordan.

"Hey, did I hurt your feelings?" Sarah's tone softened as she gazed at her friend.

Rainy leaned her elbows on the table and placed her chin beneath her palms. "No, I'm just upset because I think you're right. That being the case, it still doesn't change the way I feel for Winston. I felt connected with him and I felt he was the right man for me."

"He could be the mate God intended for you, but I can sense it's going to be a while before you find out." Sarah paused and sipped her coffee. "So, you two are just going to be friends for now?"

Rainy sighed as she crumpled the oily bags. "I guess so, but I haven't told you the worst part yet." She mentioned her accusing him of drinking.

"You didn't! Do you think that's why he doesn't think it will work between you two?"

She shrugged. "I don't know, maybe. Winston is hiding something from me, and while Winston and I work together on the church ministry, I plan on finding out what it is," she vowed.

Rainy folded the papers for the bank field trip and placed them in her purse. Children's voices echoed in the corridor, full of excitement. Winston pounded on the closed door of the empty classroom of Friendship Community Church. "Rainy, are you in there?"

She sighed, zipping her purse shut. *This is the second week of the youth financial seminars and I'm still in the dark about why Winston wanted to stop dating me. Why did I agree to do these seminars with him?* She patted her hair and opened the door.

He glanced at her, his hazel eyes full of curiosity. "What are you doing in there by yourself? The school bus just arrived to take us to the bank."

"I'm coming." She grabbed her hat and followed him out of the building into the parking lot. Being around Winston was wearing her down, and she had to take a few moments to compose herself.

Several children's voices mingled in raucous laughter as she led them to the school bus. The blistering heat scorched her skin. She pulled a large sunhat over her head and licked her dry lips as she stepped onto the vehicle.

Clara, a ten-year-old girl with dusty-brown plaits

and tiny freckles on her cinnamon-brown skin grinned at Rainy, showing the dimples in her cheeks. "Mr. Winston sure is sweet on you! Is he your boyfriend or something? You two gonna get married?"

Rainy practically pushed the child onto the bus. "That's enough, Clara. You're the nosiest kid in this group. Stop asking so many questions." Rainy settled into the vinyl seat as Winston followed close behind, guiding the other kids onto the bus.

He cleared his throat. "Now listen, everybody, you know what I told you about this field trip to the bank. You're going to listen to what the bank manager has to say, and I don't want any talking or horsing around. Did you get the permission slips from your parents?"

Several brown heads bopped. One young boy named Morris removed his paper. "Yeah, my mom signed this paper, and she said I could open a savings account." He reached his tawny hand into his backpack. "She also gave me this dollar!"

Several children waved their dollars in the air. The wilted paper created a cool breeze on the stifling bus. She sighed and leaned back into her seat, closing her eyes. Minutes later, Clara sat beside her, wiggling and kicking the floor. The doors slammed shut and the driver revved the engine. Cheers filled the bus as they pulled out of the lot.

"When are we going to get there?" whined Clara.

"Don't worry, it'll only be a little while." Wads of paper and gum littered the floor. The driver chewed on a toothpick as he maneuvered the vehicle down the

North-South Expressway. Clara vacated her seat. Rainy assumed she was looking for more promising company.

Minutes later, Clara's seat was occupied by another youth. "Hi, Miss Rainy." Terry, a fifteen-year-old participant in the program, pulled a mint from her purse. "Want one?" She popped the candy into her mouth.

Rainy shook her head and gazed at the passing scenery. The windows were open and drafts of wind plunged into the bus. Winston yelled from the rear, admonishing two fighting children. She rubbed her temple and reached into her purse. She popped two aspirins and swallowed them dry.

"You know, Miss Rainy," she said, chewing her candy, "I think you look mighty tired. Didn't you sleep last night?"

"I slept a little bit."

"Well, I think it's real nice that you and Mr. Winston let the younger people get involved in this program, too."

"Yeah, thanks to you, it is a good idea."

"After I signed up and my baby sister wanted to do the same thing, it caused a big stink in the church since this program was supposed to be for teenagers. But you and Mr. Winston said good financial skills can't start too early."

The children ranged in age from five to seventeen. She smiled as she recalled Winston's crusade to include the younger members of the parish in the youth program. At times, she forgot he was not a member of her church.

Terry nodded as she opened the package for another mint. "Mr. Winston is real smart, too. I've really learned a lot. This is only the second week we're meeting, and I'm already opening my own savings account!"

"Your boyfriend Michael didn't want to join the youth financial seminars?"

Terry shook her head as she crunched her mint. "My man doesn't need guidance when it comes to money. He's got his act together and when it's time for him to go to college, I'm sure he'll get a scholarship. Plus he works at McDonald's on Saturdays, so he can't come. He's supposed to be meeting me at the church later on today."

Excited voices mingled with the loud engine of the battered school bus. A spitball fight ensued and Winston stomped down the aisle, confiscating straws and strips of paper.

"He sure does know how to handle a bunch of kids. You probably would have had a hard time handling this project by yourself."

Winston threw the items into the trash. As he returned to his seat, he glanced at Rainy. His stormy expression softened. As he parted his full lips, a sobbing child pulled his leg. "Mr. Winston, he hit me!" She pointed her brown finger to the culprit. Winston turned to settle the dispute.

The bus jolted to a stop in front of the bank. Rainy stood and yawned while Winston herded the kids out the bus. She clutched the straps of her black leather purse as she followed the group into the bank. As the air-conditioning washed the heat from her body, she relished the cool temperature. Sweat trickled down her spine as the bank manager introduced himself.

"Now, I need to shake each of your hands since you're going to be my customers from now on. That's how we establish good business relationships." Chuckles rolled through the room as he shook hands with each small customer. "Now, let's begin our tour, shall we?"

The manager waved his hand toward the walls. "Look at the pictures lining these walls. This one is the president of the bank. You'll also see pictures of past presidents and the bank's founder."

Morris raised his copper-brown hand. "Mister, how come you don't have any black pictures on these walls? You mean you've never hired any black presidents?" His short dreadlocks danced in the air as he tilted his head toward the offending wall. Rainy sighed and rolled her eyes. She didn't know Morris's parents very well, but several members in the congregation commented that they were militant. Before Winston could respond, she pulled Morris aside, allowing the bank manager to resume his speech. His pale skin developed a rose hue as he spoke of how the prominent bank got started.

"Morris, we'll talk about this later. Right now we need to teach you kids about finances. It's the work that God has called me and Winston to do. Your attitude is not helping matters much."

"Miss Rainy, I don't mean no disrespect, but why couldn't we have put our money into a black bank?" His large brown eyes softened as he gazed at her.

"Morris, Winston and I went to just about every bank in the immediate area, and this was the only one willing to take on this project. Now listen to the manager and I'm sure you'll learn something." She paused, thinking about what she should say. "You'll be able to learn financing skills to pass on to others in the black community. When you grow up, you can start your own bank."

"Yeah, right." He folded his skinny arms.

"You can do just about anything you set your mind to do, Morris. That's what Winston taught on the first lesson, remember? Have faith in God and yourself, and things will fall into place." She pulled him toward the crowd of touring kids. "Let's rejoin the presentation, and remember to listen."

The manager continued walking around the carpeted area while showing them deposit slips and other papers. The safe-deposit boxes were next and as she stood in the cramped corner with Winston, she smelled his distinctive cologne. The children took turns entering the small chambers. Winston grazed his finger across her arm. "Are you okay?"

She swallowed and managed to nod while checking her watch.

He touched her shoulder. "Are you anxious to get out of here? That's the third time you've checked your watch since this tour has started."

She rubbed her sweaty palms against her blue jeans. Being around Winston was like sitting next to a luscious piece of chocolate cake while dieting. Her mouth watered for his kisses. She turned away as she felt the tears brimming in her eyes. She blinked and left the cramped quarters.

The bank bustled with activity. Several customers entered and stared at the group of children. The manager took them behind the teller stations, and the children's eyes bulged as they saw the wads of money being handled by the adept workers. He answered questions about banking and budgeting skills, and several of the younger children boasted about the knowledge they learned from Winston and Rainy. Harried tellers and the bank manager filled out the paperwork for the new savings accounts.

"Okay, I think you have everything." The manager shook both Winston's and Rainy's hands. "If you know of any churches who are interested in this program, just send them to me. I like to think I'm helping children to learn good money skills early in life," he said with a shaky laugh.

Winston cleared his throat. "We're sorry about Morris. He can be kind of militant sometimes."

Rainy nodded.

The manager placed his arms behind his back. "Oh, don't worry about it. I've already forgotten about it."

The children's yells echoed in the hot summer breeze as they walked across the scorching asphalt parking lot. The bus driver stood in front of the bus, inhaling from his cigarette. Smoke curled from his mouth as he took another hit.

Clara boldly rushed up to him. "Don't you know

smoking's bad for your health? God doesn't like cigarettes, mister. They make you die."

Winston pulled Clara on the bus as the driver glared at the children. "Clara, you need to learn to keep quiet. Get on this bus so we can go home!"

"But I just wanted to tell that man it's not okay to smoke. What's wrong with that?" She pulled away from Winston and stomped to the back of the bus. Minutes later, the driver returned to his seat and slammed the door shut. Giggles and laughter filled the air as the children conversed. After Winston gave a speech about good behavior on the drive home, he took the empty seat beside Rainy.

"Whew, what a rough day. If I'd have known it would be so difficult, I never would have scouted to arrange for this field trip." She stared at the way his black jeans hugged his trim thighs before gazing out the window as the driver revved the engine.

"Vroom, vroom," chanted small voices from the rear of the bus.

Once they were back on the freeway, Winston sighed. "So how have you been?"

I've been terrible since you decided we should just be friends. "I've been okay. I've been busy at work, and doing other things." The awkward silence stretched between them like a great expanse of nothingness. When a heated argument ensued at the rear of the bus, Winston abandoned his seat to resume his role as referee. Several children climbed into Winston's vacated seat, trying to ensnare her in conversation, but she just wasn't in the mood to talk. She wanted to return home, curl up in her bed and go to sleep.

Finally, the bus screeched to a stop at the church. "Lunchtime," chanted the children as they exited the bus.

Winston yelled at the bunch as they ran to the church. "Don't be running too fast! There are cars coming in this lot!" They barely paid him any attention as they opened the glass doors and ran down the stairs to the basement.

Winston followed Rainy into the building. "Are you sure you're okay with us doing this project together? You've hardly said two words all morning." His deep hazel eyes pleaded with her as he awaited her response.

You mean I've barely said two words to you *this morning.* "I'm fine. I'm just hungry. I didn't have anything for breakfast."

He nodded as he opened the door that led to the kitchen basement. They trampled down the steps as the echo of children's voices filled the corridor.

Sister Mary, the official of the church's food ministry, met them at the basement entrance. "I'm so glad to see you two finally made it back." She embraced both of them before tying an apron around her ample, bulky frame. "Rainy, you look like your best friend died! What's wrong, sweetie?" Sister Mary gave her another hug.

Rainy shrugged as she pulled out a chair and sat at the long table. Children scurried around the vast space. Some stopped to show the kitchen sisters their new bankbooks and deposit slips. "I don't know. I guess I'm just hungry."

Sister Mary pulled a rag from her pocket and wiped her face. "Well, after you two get some food in your bellies, you'll both be looking as good as new. You don't look so good yourself, Winston. Maybe you need a good meal, too. Sit down here next to Rainy and me and the kitchen sisters will handle this bunch. Remember what you guys agreed to do?"

Rainy nodded as she set her purse on the table. "We'll clean up after the children are finished eating."

Mary nodded as she bustled to the kitchen. "That's right! We've got plenty of spaghetti and garlic bread left over from today's new-member-orientation luncheon. There's also salad. After we serve these kids, we're leaving because we're tired." She turned toward the screaming kids. "Be quiet! I want all of you to stand in a line. Brother Winston will say grace and then you will make your plates and eat."

As Rainy bowed her head and listened to Winston's prayer, memories of the cruise ship meals filled her mind. She gently pushed the sweet thoughts from her brain as Winston uttered, "Amen."

She swallowed and whispered her response, as did the children. Aromas of tomatoes, garlic and spices filled the room with their tangy scent. The sisters dished up mouthwatering plates of spaghetti. They also served tall glasses of Kool-Aid. She sat beside Winston as she enjoyed two plates of the hearty meal with a few pieces of crunchy garlic bread. The grape Kool-Aid tasted good and sweet as it traveled down her parched throat.

Winston leaned his elbows on the table and smiled. Rainy's heart thundered when she discovered he was smiling at her! "You look happy when you eat. Did you enjoy the meal?"

She nodded as she toyed with a napkin. "People in the congregation say Sister Mary makes the best spaghetti."

"It's the best spaghetti I've had in a while." He leaned back into the chair and patted his stomach. "You know, that's one thing I like about you. You can enjoy a good meal and have a good time. I love watching you eat." Her heart continued to pound as he pressed his finger along her lower lip and swiped stray sauce away. She blinked as she stared into his hazel eyes. The kitchen sisters, the children and the plates of food were momentarily forgotten as she gazed at the man that she loved. She pushed her chair away from the table. Loved? Did she really love Winston? What a frightening thought!

"Rainy, what's the matter?" The noise from a blaring car horn filtered into the basement. The children scrambled from their seats and ran across the tiled floor.

"I think that's my mother! She told me I'd better be waiting outside," exclaimed one child.

Sister Mary removed her apron as she approached. "You'll find everything for cleanup in the kitchen. It shouldn't take you too long," she told Winston and Rainy. Her heavy footsteps could be heard as she ambled out of the basement.

Parents arrived to pick up their children. Soon, the only ones left in the messy kitchen were Rainy, Winston and Terry. Terry paced the floor. "I can't wait for Michael to get here! We've got an important date today." She gazed at her watch again.

Minutes later, a tall, slender young man with hazelnut-brown skin entered the basement. "Michael!" Terry ran into his arms and they shared a deep kiss. Rainy turned away and opened a box of trash bags. The young couple seemed to be in a world of their own as they planned their time.

After a whispered discussion, Michael pulled the keys from the pockets of his baggy jeans. "Come on, Terry. Let me take you home." He smiled and jiggled his keys.

As they shared another kiss, Winston pried them apart. "Why don't you two help Rainy and I clean up this mess?"

Michael kept his arm around his girlfriend. "We would stay, Mr. Winston, but I promised my mom I would be home in plenty of time to help with the yard work." He checked his watch. "If I'm not home soon, she's gonna get really mad!" Their excited voices filled the corridor as they walked up the steps, leaving Winston and Rainy alone.

"You know, I'm worried about those two," he commented.

She pulled paper plates and cups from the table and threw them into trash bags. "I know. Me, too."

"How long have they been dating?" He poured himself a cup of Kool-Aid.

She shrugged as she wrapped leftover cake with plastic wrap. "I don't know. Until we started this program, I never really worked much with the kid. From what I can remember, they've been seeing each other for months now."

She placed the cake into the refrigerator and he dumped empty soda cans and bottles into the recycling bin. After placing the bins in the corner, he gazed at the couple through the window as they strolled to Michael's car.

"Terry is a good young woman. Her parents raised her in a Christian home, and I'm sure she wouldn't do anything with Michael to shame herself," said Rainy.

He drank his Kool-Aid and threw the empty paper cup into her trash bag. He was so close that she could smell his cologne. As they continued to clean the tables, he cupped her cheek with his large hand. She dropped the plastic bag and languished the soft warm feelings as he stroked her cheek with his finger. He then abruptly dropped his hand and turned away. *I'm such a fool for letting him get to me like that! Why can't he learn to keep his hands to himself?*

"I'm sorry, I couldn't resist touching you. Your skin is so soft, it reminds me of warm butter."

She swallowed and lifted her trash bag. For several minutes, the only sound was their light footsteps as they traveled the room, collecting trash. Friends didn't touch and caress one another like that. She sighed and her heartbeat returned to normal as he changed the subject.

"Back to Terry and Michael. I'm just saying that

sometimes when things happen, it's not as if people meant for them to happen, if you know what I mean?"

Nodding, she continued her cleaning duties. "Yeah, I know what you mean."

"What do you think we should do?"

She placed her loaded trash bag into a receptacle and walked into the kitchen. She dampened a rag at the sink and returned to the adjoining dining area, answering him as she wiped the tables clean of debris. "I guess we can pray about it. I know both sets of parents know of their relationship, and they must approve. Michael is a decent young man, and his parents are involved in the church."

"Rainy…"

"I know, I know. It's still cause for worry. I do know they're together a lot, so I know they're close. We'll just have to pray that they don't make a mistake."

"They might have already made one."

She pushed her rag aside and joined him at the table. "What do you mean?"

"Remember the first financial planning meeting we had last Saturday? Well, you left early, so I helped the deacon to lock up. When we left, we saw a car parked in the lot, and it was Michael's. The windows were steamy, so you can guess what they were doing."

She gasped. "But it was the middle of the day! Wasn't it?"

He chuckled. "I'm sure Michael doesn't mind what time of day it is as long as he's with Terry. Anyway, Deacon Barnes knocked on the window and told them to hightail it home before he called their parents. Do you know if there are other young couples who've run into trouble?"

She gazed at the ceiling as she tried to remember. "There were a few unplanned pregnancies last year. Both girls had their babies. One of them kept her baby, and the other placed hers up for adoption. Unplanned pregnancies have not been an issue discussed in our small conservative church. The preacher says premarital sex is wrong, so there's no need to have further discussion about it."

"Well, maybe when the other young people see what some of the effects of premarital sex can be, then they'll reconsider being sexually active." He folded his arms across his broad chest.

"Are you going to become a member of this church? You're so involved already."

His Adam's apple bobbed as he swallowed. "No, I'm not saying I'm becoming a member. I'm just saying that Terry and Michael need to be careful about what they do when they're alone. You know, I wasn't saved when I was his age, so I'm aware of the dangers of premarital sex when you're young like that."

"So did you get somebody pregnant when you were that age?"

"No, but I came pretty close a few times. You know how hard it is to plan for those types of things…." His brown eyes widened as he gazed at her. "Or maybe you don't? I know this is none of my business, but have you ever had a pregnancy scare? I have and I was relieved when it turned out to be a false alarm."

She walked to the sink and rinsed out her rag. The basement recreation room still smelled like spaghetti sauce and garlic bread. She returned to the table. "You're right, it is none of your business. You revoked the right to know about the intimate details of my personal life when you ended our romantic involvement."

She threw the rag onto the table, but before she could stalk away, Winston grabbed her shoulder. "I didn't end our romantic involvement. I just said we should just be friends for now."

She pushed his hand away. "Well, I don't want to talk about my personal life right now. As far as you and I are concerned, I just think we need to work on this financial planning seminar project because I honestly believe the Lord called us to serve the church this way. Our friendship, relationship or whatever you want to call it doesn't need discussion. It just needs a whole lot of prayer."

He threw his hands into the air. "Don't get so hyped up." Voices, lifted in spiritual song, streamed down the basement steps. "Is choir practice going on?"

She shook her head. "No. That's the singles' ministry. Rachel and Sarah should be up there. They always start the meeting with a song."

He grinned as he walked to the foot of the steps. "I like Sarah and Rachel. I'm glad I've been able to meet them since I've been spending time at this church. I admire the bond the three of you share."

"Yeah, we're pretty close. If I had biological sisters, I'd want them to be just like Sarah and Rachel. Did you want to go to the singles' ministry meeting? It usually lasts a few hours."

He nodded as he started walking up the steps. "Yeah, why not? We're done cleaning, and I'd like to meet some more members in your church."

She gazed at the corded muscles peeking through his thin T-shirt as she followed him up the steps.

Chapter Ten

When Rainy returned home after the singles' ministry meeting, she lay on the couch to take a short nap. The phone rang, shattering the silence. She groaned, wondering if she should let the answering machine take the call. She reluctantly abandoned the comfortable couch and answered the phone. "Hello," she managed to say.

"Rainy, have you been working too hard again?" Her mother's strong voice carried over the wire, and Rainy felt like she was five years old again.

"Mom, hi."

"We haven't spoken to you in over a week. I told your father you were probably busy at your job and at your church. That congregation keeps you busy, doesn't it?"

"Yeah, Mom. How's Dad doing?"

"Oh, he's fine. He's out in the barn with Mark. One of the cows is calving tonight."

She recalled the late nights her father would some-times spend in the barn, waiting for a new cow to be born. "How are Amber, Mark and Cindy?" Her brother Mark was married and they had a three-year-old daugh-ter. She had a good relationship with the tyke, in spite of the distance in their living arrangements.

"Little Amber is fine." Her mother brought her up-to-date on the family. However, she could hear an ap-prehensive tone in her voice. Her mother sighed, and she knew something was wrong.

"Mom, what is it? I sense that something is on your mind."

"Well, I'm not really sure what the problem is, but I think Mark and Cindy are having trouble."

"Trouble? You mean in their marriage?"

She paused. "Yes. I want to talk to them about it, but I don't want to interfere."

"This is the second time this has happened in the past year. Have they talked to Pastor John? He used to help a lot of people in our congregation." She recalled the kind words married couples used to say about the pas-tor's advice. He always said his advice came straight from the Good Book, but she sensed that he had a gift when it came to dealing with couples.

"I'm not sure." Her mother paused again, seemingly wondering if she should say more. Rainy heard the door open and her father enter the house. Soon he had taken the phone from her mother.

"Hi, Miss Rainy!" her father boomed. After she had talked to him for a few minutes, she finally got off of the phone. Before she went to bed that night, she said a quick prayer for her brother's marriage. Mark and Cindy seemed to be made for each other. Hopefully their problems would be fixed soon.

Rainy spent the next few weeks praying for her brother's marriage, hoping he could work things out with his wife. When she had weekly lunches with Sarah and Rachel, she brought them up-to-date on her prayer requests, and she also told them about how hard it was to work with Winston every Saturday, while still not knowing why he suddenly ended their courtship.

She looked forward to seeing him every Saturday morning as his deep voice outlined basic financial skills to the church youth. However, too soon, it was time for the seminars to come to a close.

On the last day of the seminar, she struggled to open her eyes. When she finally managed to awaken, she witnessed the bright fingers of sunlight spilling into her bedroom, illuminating the floral design on her favorite blue comforter. She blinked, still trying to clear her groggy mind. She snuggled beneath her blanket as she listened to the birds welcome in the new day. She was due at the church soon.

She sighed as she closed her eyes, relishing the warmth of her cocoon of blankets. She finally pulled herself out of bed and stumbled into the kitchen. As the coffee brewed, she wondered how she would survive another Saturday morning in Winston's company.

Since it was the final session of the Youth Financial

Program at Friendship Church, she felt torn. She was glad that she could end this weekly torture of seeing Winston without fulfilling their relationship—she also felt sad to see the program end. The thought of never seeing him again made her heart pound with trepidation. She took a deep breath as she said a silent prayer, asking the Lord for strength.

A few hours later she wandered the grounds of Friendship Community Church. Children ran around long picnic tables, shrieking with laughter.

She grinned at Sister Mary as she served another burger to a hungry child. *Sister Mary can master anything to do with cooking.* She gazed at the crowd of excited kids, teenagers and parents, seeking one person. She watched Michael as he stood away from the crowd with Terry. She wished there was something she could do to help the young couple. Winston's apprehensions had proven to be merited. Terry was now pregnant with her first child.

She walked around the picnic area, still seeking her financial advisory partner. She spotted Sarah and Rachel as they helped some of the older kids to organize a Biblical trivia game. She waved at her best friends, pleased they agreed to help with the Youth Financial Advisory Picnic.

When she still couldn't find Winston, she finally entered the sanctuary of the church. High-pitched screams filtered through the stained-glass windows. The tension eased from her body when she spotted Winston in the foyer, speaking to one of the parents. She walked into the sanctuary, deciding to approach him later. She sat on the cushioned seat and closed her eyes, relishing the cool temperature.

"Rainy, what's wrong?" Winston sat beside her in the empty pew.

His blue jeans hugged his firm thighs and his cologne smelled tangy and enticing. Her heart pounded and her palms became moist. Would being this close to Winston always have this effect on her? She wondered if they would ever recapture the closeness they had shared on the cruise.

"Oh, nothing…everything." Her voice shook as she leaned back into the pew.

"Well, tell me about it," he urged as he caressed her shoulder. Her skin sizzled from his touch and she moved away. Since when had Winston become her confidant? He'd been so standoffish since they began working together that she wondered if she'd imagined the fun they'd shared on the cruise.

"Look." He touched her arm again. "You know we're friends, right?"

Friends? At this point, she hated using that word when it came to Winston. She wanted to be more than just a friend.

"If you want to call it that," she said sarcastically.

"Rainy…" He sounded so tired, and she didn't feel like arguing. She had too much on her mind.

"I'm going home in a few weeks."

"Really? I'm assuming this isn't an ordinary visit?"

"No, it isn't." When he protectively placed his arm

around her, her apprehensions disappeared. She settled into his comforting embrace as she told of the conversations she'd had with her mother over the past week.

"So, your brother's wife had an affair, and now she's left him? That's rough." He toyed with her fingers.

She nodded. "I knew they'd been having problems, but I thought they'd work them out. I never suspected Cindy would have an affair." It was a shocking thought, and she still found it all so hard to believe. She still felt like she was in the middle of a bad dream, and all she wanted to do was awaken.

"They have a daughter, right?"

She nodded, pleased that he remembered so much about her family. "I feel bad for Amber. She's so little. That's one reason why I think I should go home for a few days. My father is beside himself, running that dairy farm. Mark is so depressed that he's not much help."

"Your family is important to you, aren't they?"

Nodding, she settled into the crook of his arm and closed her eyes.

Winston fingered Rainy's long dark hair, wondering if she would be offended if he placed his lips against her temple. Thoughts of kissing her cluttered his mind until her sweet voice silenced his reverie.

She opened her large dark eyes and looked at him. "Did you talk to Michael and Terry?"

He nodded. "Yes, I did as a matter of fact. Michael told me everything."

She sighed, pulling herself from his embrace. "Terry talked to me. I guess you were right to be concerned about them."

"Yeah, I recall your telling me that your preacher says that abstinence is the key to avoiding unplanned pregnancies. I wish Michael and Terry could have followed his advice." He was silent for a few minutes. "You know, this is a terrible way for them to start the new school year."

"I agree with you. All we can do is keep them in our prayers." Heavy footsteps pounded on the cranberry-colored carpet.

He noticed the pastor approaching. He loomed over them, carrying a manila folder. "Hi, Reverend Marshall," Winston greeted.

"Hi, Rainy, hi, Winston." He lowered his bulky frame into the pew and embraced Rainy before shaking Winston's hand. Stroking his salt-and-pepper beard, Reverend Marshall's eyes glowed with warmth and mischief as he gazed at them. "I just want you two to know that the whole congregation has been buzzing about the success of the Youth Financial Program. This is the first time this church has sponsored such an event for our youth, and it's turned out quite nicely." Staring at the empty pulpit, he continued his speech. "You know, you two work so well together that I want you to think about something for me, possibly pray about it."

Rainy touched his arm. "What is it you want us to pray about, Reverend?"

"Well, number one, a lot of the youth look up to you, Winston. I wanted to know if you'd consider being a member of this church. I do realize you have your own church home, but you could become an associate member and then pray about becoming a full member."

"Reverend," Winston began.

"Just think about it, Winston. You don't have to give me your answer now."

He nodded. "Okay, I'll think about it."

Reverend Marshall looked at Rainy. "What's the matter, Rainy? You don't like my idea?"

"I'm not sure if it's a good idea, Reverend."

"Well, you two work so well together, and I just assumed you'd want to continue serving the church in this manner."

Winston frowned. "Uh, did I miss something? Continue serving the church in this manner?"

Reverend Marshall nodded. "Of course. Rainy, I'm sure you recall that Deacon Thomas, who used to head the children's ministry, has moved away. Well, I figured you and Winston would be perfect candidates to replace him. You've done so well with the Youth Financial Seminar, and I'm sure you'll do well with the children's ministry. The next big event they've got scheduled is the Christmas Pageant. I know it's only the beginning of September, but this is the largest children's event in the church, and it takes lots of planning and preparation. Hopefully the two of you will see it in your hearts to take this on."

The Reverend stood and squeezed Winston's shoulder. "I hope you'll let me know as soon as possible. If the two of you aren't interested, then we'll have to ask somebody else in the congregation to take on this project." His large feet plodded down the aisle before he stopped and turned toward them. "Oh, let me know within a couple of weeks. That'll give you some time to think about it and pray about it. I feel in my heart that the Lord has called both of you to work with the children in this church."

Winston whistled softly. "Mercy, I never would have expected this to happen today. I thought our involvement in the Youth Financial Seminar was the end of our calling, but looks like I was wrong."

Rainy gasped, shoving his shoulder. "You've got to be kidding. Do you honestly think it would be a good idea for you to join this church, and for us to work together in the children's ministry?"

Winston remained silent as he stared at the large cross in the pulpit. *Lord, what have You called me to do?*

Winston spent the rest of the picnic in a daze, wondering how he should plan his church activities in the future. He watched Rainy as she helped Sister Mary serve the hungry children. He admired her easy camaraderie with her friends, Sarah and Rachel. At one point, the three girlfriends sat under a large oak tree, laughing wildly. Rainy looked up and caught him staring, so he quickly looked away.

He watched Rainy from afar for the rest of the day.

He wanted to take her away from this crowd and spend some time alone with her, on a real date. His heart skipped a beat when she finally left the picnic, without even looking his way or saying goodbye. The church grounds were growing empty, and the cleanup crew was removing the debris left behind.

He trudged to his car, wondering how he would spend his Saturday night. He suddenly felt lonely, and he knew he would miss the joy and camaraderie he'd found in Rainy's church—but most of all, he knew he would miss Rainy.

As he drove, he barely paid attention to the passing traffic and the beautiful palm trees dotting the side of the road. Waves of loneliness continued to engulf him, and he suddenly didn't want to go home and be by himself. He made a U-turn and drove toward his aunt Gladys's house. He pulled into the driveway as gospel music drifted through her open windows. He knocked, and his aunt yelled for him to come inside.

She sat in a rocking chair, knitting. A spool of crimson yarn was strewn around her lap and a pair of reading glasses perched on her nose. "Winston, what in the world are you doing here?" She placed her knitting aside as he kissed her cheek. Since the music continued to blare from the stereo, he turned it down.

He shrugged as he sat on the tattered floral-patterned couch. "What's wrong with a visit to my favorite aunt?"

"Humph. This ain't no friendly visit."

He playfully placed his hands over his chest. "Aunt Gladys, I'm hurt. Why wouldn't this be a friendly visit?"

"Boy, I've known you since the day you were born. I can tell by that sad look on your face that you've got something on your mind and you just needed to talk to somebody about it. What are you so upset about anyway? Does it have anything to do with that girl you told me about? The one you met on the cruise ship?"

Before he could answer, she scurried to the kitchen and returned with a plate of frosted chocolate brownies. "Here, have one of these. You always liked my brownies when you were feeling low about something."

He removed one of the dark squares and popped it into his mouth whole. When he was finished, he reached for another. "Hey, these are great! You even put macadamia nuts in them."

"Now, boy, tell me what's on your mind," she demanded, ignoring the compliment.

"You can certainly read me like a book. Yes, this has something to do with Rainy."

"What's the matter?" She selected a brownie and sat back in her chair.

He sighed, finishing off another brownie. "Well, you know that Youth Financial Seminar that I was doing with Rainy?"

She continued to give him her full attention. "Why, yes. I think it was mighty fine the way you two have been spending your Saturday afternoons helping those young people. I'm really proud of you."

"Thanks," he mumbled. "My problem is Rainy. I already told her that we could just be friends, and I really liked seeing her every weekend while we did the seminars together."

Gladys shrugged. "But?"

"I really like Rainy…a lot. And I don't know how I'm going to manage not seeing her each week anymore. I want us to date again, and be more than just friends, but I don't think that'll be a good idea." He then told her of Pastor Marshall's offer for them to lead the children's ministry.

She folded her arms in front of her chest. "What's the matter with you? She lives right here in Miami, so there's no reason for you not to date this girl."

He stared at his aunt. "You know why I can't date Rainy."

"No, I don't." Her mouth was set in a firm line.

He sighed. "You know about my drinking problem. I can't put Rainy through that."

"You've been sober since Pam died, that should amount for something. Plus, you need to remember the faith you have in Jesus. Lean on Him and He'll show you what to do."

She resumed her knitting, seemingly dismissing him from further conversation. *Why is she acting so mad at me?*

He glanced around the house. "Uh, where's Uncle Greg?" he asked, changing the subject.

Her knitting needles clattered as she answered, "He's out with some people from the church. He should be back in about an hour or so if you wanted to wait for him."

"No, I think it's time for me to leave."

As he opened the door, her voice stopped him in his tracks. "You just remember what I told you. You keep forgetting you need to lean on God, and you should be honest with Rainy about how you feel. Don't be a coward. You really like this girl, and it's not right to turn your back on that because of your fears."

The screen door banged shut as he left the house and returned to his car. He drove around in the semidarkness until he reached Rainy's small home. The porch light was on, illuminating the oak rocking chair and iron lawn furniture.

He sniffed the scent of the orange trees planted at the side of the road. The sweet smell filled his nostrils as he watched her house. "Lord, what am I doing here?" He turned his radio on to a gospel station. He made sure the volume was low as he listened to the sweet melody about the death of Jesus Christ.

He leaned back into his car seat and continued to stare out of the window. He opened his sunroof and gazed at the bright stars twinkling in the semidark sky. "Lord, why am I here?" he asked softly. "Please show me a sign, let me know if I'm strong enough to be a good man for Lorraine Jackson," he pleaded. "I don't want to fall into the trap of alcoholism again. I don't want to be a failure to her."

He continued to gaze at the sky. "Rainy has suffered enough. She's a strong, proud woman and I don't want to hurt her. Is it best if we stay just friends, or should I pursue her as a future mate? Please help me out, here,

Lord," he paused and swallowed. "Please show me what I need to do. Amen," he whispered. He closed his eyes for a brief moment, and his burden seemed to lift in the slight breeze moving through the orange trees.

Show her how you feel. His heart skipped a beat as he wondered if God was answering his prayers in a meaningful way. *Patience is a virtue. Be patient with her and show her how you feel.* He sighed with relief as he opened his eyes.

"Yes, Lord, I'll show Rainy how I feel. I'll be a patient man, and maybe things will work out between us."

Rainy was still thinking about the Youth Financial Advisory Picnic as she pulled her laundry out of the dryer. She'd caught Winston staring at her all day, and she wondered if it was a sign that things could work out for them after all.

After doing numerous household chores, she finally went to bed, exhausted. Dreams of Winston plagued her sleep and when she woke up the following morning, she felt far from being refreshed.

During the early-morning church service, she struggled to stay awake and listen to the sermon, and when she happened to scan the parishioners, she spotted Winston sitting in one of the pews near the front!

Her stomach was tied in knots when she saw him talking to Sarah and Rachel in the foyer after the service. Minutes later, he approached her, requesting that they spend time together that afternoon.

Her mouth was as dry as a ball of cotton. "But I have plans with Sarah and Rachel after church."

He grinned as his fingers grazed her cheek. "I already talked to them and they know you'll be spending the afternoon with me."

She went home and changed, and Winston arrived minutes after she was finished.

His car sparkled from being recently washed and the windows shined beneath the hot afternoon sun. Rainy folded her arms over her chest. "Where are we going?"

He pulled her toward his car, kissing her cheek as he opened her car door for her. "It's a surprise, sweetheart. Don't mess it up by asking a lot of questions." His hazel eyes were full of mischief as he pulled away from her house.

Minutes later the car jolted to a stop at an exclusive deli and bistro in the heart of Miami. "What are we doing here?" She waved toward the deli. "Is this the reason why you made me change my brunch plans with Sarah and Rachel?"

He nodded. "Yep. Hold on, I'll be right back." He rushed into the deli, returning minutes later with a basket. "Lunch at your service." He slid behind the wheel. As they pulled onto the street, she opened the basket and found it was laden with all her favorite foods: Italian submarine sandwiches, onion chips, potato salad and two thick slabs of chocolate cake. There was also a bottle of sparkling cider and two glasses.

"This is so sweet!" She gazed at the luscious meal. Her mouth watered and her empty stomach growled.

"Oh, so you're hungry, huh?" He tousled her hair as she placed the basket into the back seat.

"Where are we going?" she repeated as she gazed at the palm trees dotting the side of the road.

"Well, I'm sure you saw me talking to Sarah and Rachel after the service. They told me what I needed to do to plan this special meal for you."

Minutes later they entered the state park. A few families frolicked in the grass, and a boy was playing Frisbee with his dog. But otherwise, it wasn't too crowded. She quickly exited the car, and when Winston opened the trunk, he produced an old faded quilt. "My aunt Gladys gave this to me years ago. It comes in handy when I need to eat outside." They walked to the edge of a sparkling brook and watched the clear water rush over the smooth stones. She tilted her head toward the sky, enjoying the sunshine.

He took her hands and caressed her fingers. "Can we pray first?"

She smiled and nodded. They bowed their heads together, their foreheads touching. "Lord, please help Rainy's family during this difficult time. Please help her brother Mark with his problems, and please keep Rainy and Amber safe in their days to come. We thank you for this lovely day, and I thank You, Lord, for allowing me to meet Lorraine Jackson on a cruise ship four months ago. Amen."

"Amen," she whispered. She missed the warmth of his touch as he released her hands. "I'm so glad that you prayed for my family. Thank you," she whispered.

"I know how important your family is to you. You seemed upset when you found out about your brother's problems."

As they enjoyed their food, she couldn't recall the last time she'd had such a lavish picnic. As they toyed with their glasses of sparkling cider, she touched his arm. "What's all this about?" She gestured toward the empty picnic basket. "You get my favorite foods and you take me to my favorite picnic spot. I know you said a while ago that you just wanted us to be friends, but this afternoon it feels like you want to be more than just friends." She took a sip of her cider and enjoyed the tangy sweetness on her tongue.

He removed her cider from her hand and set both glasses under a tree. She enjoyed the warmth and support from his hard chest as he took her into his arms and she leaned against him. She closed her eyes and relished the brush of his firm lips against her temple. "What does this mean?" she asked again. Had he changed his mind?

He stiffened for a moment, but he relaxed as he tightened his grip around her waist. "There's just so much I want to say, but I just don't know how you'll react to it all."

She sighed as she sniffed his citrus-scented cologne. "Tell me everything. I want to know what happened between us. Why did you decide you wanted us to just be friends?"

The breath of his sigh traveled over her heated skin. Being this close to him made her feel hot and cold at the same time.

"Oh, a few things. First off, I wasn't sure if you were over Jordan. You were grieving over your loss on the cruise, plus I saw you having dinner with him at Raymond's. I know we dated for a few months after that, but I figured since you'd been in love with him before, chances were, you might take him back."

"I won't go back to Jordan! Not now! I only had dinner with him because he kept pursuing me, and it was the only way to get him off my back. We discussed this when you grilled hot dogs for me in the park."

She removed herself from his arms and faced him on the blanket. "Is that the only reason you wanted us to be friends?"

"Well, no, but that was a big part of it." He paused. "Is Jordan still in the picture? Do you still talk to him?"

She folded her arms and glared into his hazel-brown eyes. "What difference would it make to you? You said you just wanted to be friends." She turned away and he grabbed her arm.

"Please don't be mad. I'm trying to make everything right. I know it's going to take some time, but give me credit for trying." He gestured toward their picnic.

"I'm sorry. I'm just trying to understand you, that's all."

"I'm glad you're trying, really, I am." He released her arm and she crossed her legs as she waited for him to continue.

"Just tell me if Jordan will be an obstacle. Because if you still have feelings for him, then I'm going to need to know."

She sighed as she gazed at him. "No, Jordan and I are finished. I have no feelings for him. I've told you this before. You're beating this whole thing into the ground and, frankly, it's getting on my nerves."

"You never see him, or talk to him?"

She sighed again. "Jordan is persistent. You know, he's been coming to my church, and he sometimes comes over to speak to me. I can't just ignore him, especially at church," she defended.

"No, you're right about that." He bit his lower lip as he continued to look at her. "I believe you."

"It's about time," she huffed. "Now can you tell me what else is bothering you?"

"You know I used to be an alcoholic."

"Yes, you told me about it on the cruise."

"Well, that's part of the reason why I didn't pursue a relationship with you. I'm scared." At that moment, he did seem as scared as a frightened child.

"What are you afraid of?" She scooted closer to him and held his hand.

He sighed as she gazed into the canopy of elongated palm tree leaves. They lifted in the fall breeze, and she relished the coolness against her skin. In his deep enthralling voice, he told her of his visit to his aunt and uncle's house several weeks ago. "Just seeing my uncle, drunk like that, reminded me of my addiction. I'm an alcoholic. Whether I touch a drop of booze or not, I'll always be an alcoholic."

"Oh, Winston." She hugged his broad torso, and relished the feel of his muscled arms. "You've just got to have some faith, that's all. You haven't had a drop of booze in a long time."

She pulled away and a frown creased his handsome features. "What's wrong?" Dread crept up her spine, but she pushed the negative feeling aside. He was hiding something. She could sense it.

"Nothing. But what if something happens? What if I get depressed like my uncle? What'll happen then? Will I turn back to my old ways?" He paused as he gazed at his hands. "I just changed my mind about our relationship after I saw my uncle's tirade. It was like a wake-up call."

"Have faith in God and everything will work out. I just know it will."

She took his hands and closed her eyes. "I'm sure the Lord will help you through this." She released his hands and opened her eyes as he reclaimed their glasses of cider. She enjoyed the tangy sweetness of the drink as it traveled down her throat.

He sipped his cider as he gazed at the sparkling brook. A dog sloshed in the water, barking fanatically.

She fingered the stem of her plastic cup, frowning.

"What's wrong?"

She sighed. "Just thinking about my family's problems. My parents are really anxious for me to come home. I think they might have something important to talk to me about."

"You mean something other than your brother's wife's affair?"

She nodded while the wind continued to blow and

her long hair whipped across her face. He playfully pushed the stray hairs behind her ear. "I think so. It's just a feeling that I have. I want to see my parents, but I'm not looking forward to going home, not under these circumstances anyway."

He pulled her into his arms and whispered in her ear. "Let me help you to forget about your problems for a minute." As his lips pressed against hers, waves of joy fluttered through her soul, calming her frazzled nerves. "Would you do me the honor of dating again? I promise I won't mess up this time." His breathing sounded labored and intense, and she tried to calm her racing heart.

Closing her eyes, she recalled the pain and disappointment she'd endured when he broke off their relationship the first time. She swallowed, as she prayed to say the right words. "Are you sure this is what you want?"

She placed some distance between them, scooting farther away from him on the blanket. She finally looked at him again, wondering what he was going to say.

He sighed, his full lips set in a grim line. "I understand why you're concerned, but since I've accepted Christ in my life, I make sure I always tell the truth. Now that you know why I was hesitant about having a relationship with you, and everything is out in the open, I feel more confident that things can work between us."

He touched her cheek, and feelings of warmth and happiness flowed through her like sweet honey.

"Sweetheart, I've missed dating you. I enjoyed working with you during the seminars, but it was hard, seeing you, and knowing that we couldn't be more than just friends."

She cleared her throat. "And now we can be more than just friends?" Her soft voice was barely audible in the large park.

"I think we can be. Please, give me a chance and we'll see how this works." He paused and gazed at the stream again. "I know you're worried about your family and all, and I'd like to be there for you while you help them to work things out."

She licked her lips as her breathing returned to normal. She closed her eyes, and said a brief prayer before giving him her response. "This is so sudden."

"I've been wanting to do this but I was scared. My aunt Gladys had to convince me that my bad attitude could ruin one of the best things in my life."

"I can't give you an answer right now," she whispered.

"How about I give you a few days to think about it?"

She nodded, her long hair swinging in the warm breeze. "Okay, I'll let you know my answer soon."

Over the next few days, Rainy's office became flooded with flowers. Roses, lilies, baby's breath and carnations exploded the small space with vibrant colors. She opened her office door and peeked into Linda's cubicle. She found another bouquet of blossoms sitting on her assistant's desk, while Linda openly read the card.

"Are these for me?" Rainy asked, snatching the card away, upset that her assistant would read the personal messages Winston had been attaching to the flowers.

Linda stood, smoothing imaginary wrinkles on her skintight red dress. She ran her long nails through her bleached platinum-blond locks. "I'm sorry, Rainy. I was just making sure they were yours before I put them in your office." She giggled, covering her full red-painted lips.

Rainy huffed, taking the flowers and card into her office. The deep perfumed scents clung to her nostrils, making her feel as if she was in the midst of an exquisite garden. Dropping into her leather chair, she pulled the cream-colored cards from her desk and read every one again. In each card, Winston proclaimed his desire for them to start dating again. She dropped the cards on her desk. While closing her eyes, she recalled the romantic days she spent with him on the cruise ship.

The loud ringing of her phone broke into her reverie. She lifted the receiver, relaying her greeting.

"Hi, Rainy." Winston's deep tone sounded hesitant. "Did you get all those flowers I sent you?"

She gazed around her cluttered office, wondering if he had gone into debt by sending her so many flowers. She sighed, twisting the phone cord between her fingers. "Yes, I got them. They're lovely." She stopped and sniffed. "And they smell nice, too."

He chuckled warmly. "I'm glad you like them. I just want you to know that I'm determined not to mess up this time. That is, if you decide to go out with me again.

It would mean so much to me if you said yes and gave me another chance. I promise I'll do my best not to mess things up."

She stroked the ivory-colored cards, pondering Winston's words. The pain in her heart could be quenched if she were in Winston's company again. Squeezing the most-recent card between her fingers, she answered his question. "Yes, I'd like for us to date again."

Winston smiled as he clutched the receiver. "You've made me a very happy man today. You don't know how much this means to me."

They talked for a few minutes, and she mentioned her dreaded trip home to see her family. He knew she wasn't too excited about making this trip, and he wished there was something he could do to make it easier for her.

He stood and sat on the corner of his desk, still listening to her speak about her family's troubles. When she finally paused, he said what was on his mind. "I want to talk to you about something."

Her voice faltered. "What did you want to talk to me about?"

"Did you need some friendly support when you go home next weekend?"

"Friendly support?"

"Yeah. Did you need somebody to lean on?"

"What are you suggesting? Did you want to give me a ride to the airport?"

"I was going to drive you to the airport and get on the plane with you. That is, if it's what you want?"

"I'm not sure if it's a good idea for you to come home with me."

He squeezed the receiver and gazed out the window to the busy city street of Miami. "Why not? We've already agreed that we're going to date again. I'm serious about being honest with you and making this work. I like you." He swallowed. "I like you a lot. I know making this trip will be difficult for you and I want to come with you if it'll make things easier for you."

"I know, but…" She paused, again. "Well, I don't know. I still don't quite understand why you would want to come."

He sighed as he ran his hand over his face. "I just explained why. I can't get any plainer than that."

He wondered what she was thinking. "Okay."

"So, I can come with you?" His heart lifted when he heard the news.

"Yes. I don't quite understand why I'm agreeing to let you come with me next weekend. I just know I'm going home, and it feels right that you should come with me."

Chapter Eleven

Rainy dragged her suitcase to the door. Scanning her living room, she made sure everything was in place. She glanced at her watch as she sank into her couch. "Where is Winston?"

Parting her yellow curtains, she looked in her driveway for his familiar car. As she continued to wait, she thought about how much her life had changed over the past week. They were officially dating, and now they were going home to her family's dairy farm. Hearing his strong voice every night on the phone before she went to bed was like music to her ears.

Minutes later, the sound of his horn blared into the room. She opened her large oak door and he strolled into the house. "How much luggage do you have?"

She pointed to the dark blue designer case. He frowned slightly as he lifted the luggage. "Is this it?"

She shrugged as she followed him outside, locking

the door behind her. "You should be pleased. I'm one of the few women on this earth who travels light." Shadows gathered in the clouds, hiding the warm sun. The only sound whispering in the early morning was their feet, crunching over the gravel driveway. He opened his trunk and deposited her suitcase beside his.

She sighed as she leaned against the seat, watching the palm and orange trees race before her window as he navigated to the Miami International Airport.

A few hours later, the plane taxied down the runway and accelerated into the sky. Once they reached their altitude, she gazed from her window, watching the ugly gray sky change to a beautiful shade of cornflower blue.

He laced his fingers through hers. "Why are you so quiet?" His deep voice was a whisper in her ear. His sweet breath smelled like mint toothpaste.

She tilted her head toward the window. "Look, isn't it beautiful?"

He glimpsed through the window. A smile touched his full lips. "That is beautiful. You know, when people doubt the existence of God, I think they just need to look around them…observe. God is good, and it's obvious when you see this beautiful earth He created."

She agreed. "Amen." They stared at the sky a few moments longer. The flight attendant approached, offering cookies and beverages. He ripped his cellophane bag and popped a few cookies into his mouth.

"You know, I'm so worried about my brother. When he married Cindy, I figured it would be for better or worse, but it looks like I was wrong. Divorce is such an ugly word, and I can't believe Mark will be going through that experience pretty soon."

He finished his snack and sipped his soda. "Are you sure there's no hope for them at all?"

"From what I hear, it's pretty grim."

"Have you talked to your brother?"

She shook her head. "No. I've just spoken to Mom and Dad. I think Mark's in pretty bad shape right now." She paused and ran her fingers through her hair. "I remember when Mark and Cindy were dating. They were so young and so much in love! I never would have believed they would have such huge marital problems. I figured their deep faith in Christ would help sustain their marriage."

He massaged her shoulder and pressed his lips to her cheek. "Don't worry so much about it. The Lord can work miracles. You never know—in due time, they might find their way back to each other again."

When they arrived at Baltimore-Washington International Airport she rented a car. Moments later, she maneuvered the vehicle onto the highway, toward her parents' dairy farm. "I know you'll be shocked when you see where I grew up." She flipped her turn signal as they exited the main highway.

He sighed as he leaned back into the seat. "Why are you so apprehensive about showing me your home? Don't you understand that it doesn't matter to me where you came from?" He paused, gazing at vast plains.

As soon as they were off of the highway, she turned onto a long winding road. An unpleasant odor filled his nostrils. There was also a nip in the air, and he snuggled into the light jacket she'd told him to bring. He closed his window. "What is that?"

"You mean the smell? You're in farm country now, so you'd better get used to it."

When she pulled into the driveway of her family's dairy farm, the smell was almost unbearable. "How can anybody get used to that stench?" Wrinkling his nose, he slowly exited the car.

An elderly woman with salt-and-pepper hair strolled down the driveway, and an elderly man followed close behind. They hugged Rainy as tears streamed down their brown cheeks. "Rainy, we're so glad you came. Things are going so bad here. We've been to Pastor John about Mark's problems. Now we're just hoping and praying things will work out." They held each other in a tight unit, and Winston toyed with the zipper on his jacket. As they continued to console one another, he opened the trunk. As he removed the luggage, they broke their embrace, and her parents gazed at him, curiosity in their cinnamon-colored eyes. *She didn't tell them that I was coming?*

Pulling his sleeve, she pushed him closer to the couple. "This is Winston."

"I'm Paul Jackson." He shared a firm handshake with Rainy's father. "I'm glad you came with our baby." Rainy rolled her eyes at his words.

Her mother approached. "I'm Constance. I'm so

glad you came." She spoke in a warm gentle tone as she enfolded him into an embrace. Her pine-and-cloves scent reminded him of his own mother.

As they walked up the steps, the cracked porch came into view. An old swing suspended on a rusty chain moved in rhythm to the suddenly howling wind. Paul was the last to enter the kitchen. "Looks like we might get a storm tonight."

Constance nodded. "I hope so. We could really use the rain for the crops."

The worn linoleum floor creaked as Winston strolled around the kitchen. "Rainy tells me this farm has been in your family for generations."

Constance nodded, a thoughtful smile curling her lips as she made a pot of coffee. "Yes, dairy farming is in this family's blood. Me and Paul love this farm." She sighed as the coffeemaker hummed and the liquid dripped into the pot. "Rainy, I just don't know what we're going to do. We've always been an upstanding, Godly family, and this is the first time something so devastating has happened to us."

Paul kneaded his wife's shoulder before hauling the suitcases upstairs.

"How is Mark holding up?" asked Rainy. The coffee stopped dripping and Winston fixed her coffee for her. He squeezed her shoulder as he sat beside her.

Paul returned to the kitchen, hearing Rainy's question. "He's been a basket case." After pouring a cup of coffee, he eased into a chair. "He barely gets up early enough to milk the cows. I've been doing the morning milking myself because he won't get up. You know how bad my joints hurt in the morning from my arthritis."

They spent the next few hours wondering what to do about Mark. Rainy glanced around the quiet house. "How's Amber?"

Constance stood at the sink, washing dirty cups. "She's been staying up here with us. We figure it'll be easier on Mark if she does. She went to bed already, but I'm sure she'll be glad to see you."

Paul placed his arm around his wife's waist. "We'll talk to you kids in the morning. I've got to get to bed. You know I've got to milk those cows early."

Constance nodded. "Say a prayer for your brother and his wife. We're still hoping things will work out between them." After they shuffled from the kitchen, Rainy and Winston strolled into the nippy night. The fallen leaves crunched beneath their feet as they walked to the barn.

Some of the cows were lying on their stomachs while others chewed their food, their tails swishing in the cool night air. Looking through the barn window, Winston gazed at the large flat plain of farmland.

He stepped away from the window and touched one of the large cows. As Rainy swept the floor, she told him about the mechanics of running a dairy farm. "It's so much hard work and like I told you on the cruise, farming is just not for me."

She placed the broom in an adjoining closet. She led him to the heifer barn and he observed the smaller cows as they slept. "What do you think will happen to the farm now? Will Mark still want to run the farm with your parents now that his wife is gone? Do you even think she'll come back?"

She shrugged her slender shoulders. "It's hard to say if Cindy will come back. I still don't quite understand what happened. I know they'd been having marriage problems since Amber's birth. When I heard about the affair, I nearly freaked out! I never suspected something that drastic would happen to them."

As they walked back to the house, he pulled her hand into his. "I brought a lot of old clothes like you suggested."

"I'm glad. Now you see why." She gestured toward the barn.

When they stepped onto the porch, he removed the shoes he'd borrowed to go to the barn. She reminded him that it was not a good idea to wear good shoes while stepping around cow manure.

Later that night, Winston tossed and turned in his sleep. Fat drops of rain plodded on the roof and thunder sounded in the sky. The wind howled all night, and he wondered if he would ever fall asleep.

The next morning, he heard a rooster crowing at the crack of dawn. He groaned as he rolled over in his bed. The mattress was as soft as cotton and the handmade quilt provided a cocoon of warmth. He heard Paul downstairs and he recalled Rainy's father saying he had been doing the morning milking since Mark had been depressed over his wife's sudden departure.

He quickly scooted out of bed, brushed his teeth and pulled on his worn jeans and faded sweater. He pulled his jacket over his broad shoulders and when he got to the kitchen, he donned the shoes he'd borrowed the previous night. He briskly walked to the barn, barely paying attention to the crisp sunny morning and the chicks scampering in their coop. He noticed Rainy's mother gathering eggs and he waved to her as he entered the barn.

Paul seemed surprised when he saw him. "Winston!" The stench of cow manure greeted him, but he didn't notice it as much as the previous day.

"I remember you saying Mark hadn't been doing the milking in the morning so I thought I'd come and help."

Paul's brown eyes crinkled with amusement as he pitched feed into the cows' tray. "Rainy didn't mention that you could milk a cow."

He grinned, hoping he wasn't making a fool of himself. "Well, I can't, but since Mark's not out here helping you, I thought I could substitute."

Paul chuckled. He spent the next few hours showing him how he did the milking. Winston did make himself useful for a while, until a cow urinated a few inches from his shoes. He jumped away, and Paul laughed. After the milking was done, he joined Paul in the adjoining room to help clean the milking equipment.

As the water ran over the cups and hoses, Paul looked thoughtful. "You know, I was surprised to see Rainy bring somebody home with her."

Winston leaned against the wall as he watched Paul do his chore. Cats skittered across the barn floor, eagerly seeking stray drops of white milk. "To tell you the truth, Mr. Jackson, Rainy didn't ask me to come. I offered. She seemed so upset, and…well, I care about her, so I wanted to come."

"You don't have to call me Mr. Jackson. Paul is fine." He turned the water off. After wiping his hands on a towel, he sat on an empty crate. Winston found another empty milk crate and sat also. He lifted one of the cats and stroked its fur. The cat purred contentedly.

"Why do you have so many cats?"

"Keeps the mice away." He lifted one of the feline creatures as they sat in comfortable silence. The cows had been led out of the barn and were in the fields, enjoying the sweet green grass. He noticed that Constance had returned to the house.

"So you care about my little girl?" Paul released the cat. He gave Winston his full attention, suddenly serious.

"Yes."

Winston sighed as he released the cat. He leaned back against the barn and the door creaked. A rooster crowed and the breeze ruffled the leaves in the trees. "You know, I think Rainy's still hurting over the way Jordan treated her."

Paul nodded. "That Jordan was a no-good…well, I'm a Christian, so profanity isn't part of my vocabulary. But that guy needed Jesus in his life. I just wish we had been able to find a way to keep them from falling in love and getting engaged. I never liked the guy, but Rainy was so smitten with him that I made the effort to accept him into our family. That's why we gave the engagement party."

He waited for Paul to continue. Rainy had never mentioned her parents' disapproving of her engagement to Jordan. "Well, I told Rainy that I had apprehensions about her relationship with Jordan, but she didn't want to hear the truth about my feelings. I had no concrete evidence about his disrespectful behavior, but you'll realize that as you get older, you just get a feel for people. And let me tell you, Jordan Summers gave me a bad feeling." He swallowed as he rested his chin in his hand. "I told Rainy that maybe she should get to know Jordan better before she accepted the ring, but she refused to listen. It got to the point that whenever she called home, we always ended up arguing about Jordan."

"What did your wife say?"

He shrugged. "What could Constance say? She just pointed out to me that she didn't disapprove of my feelings toward our daughter's fiancé, but she said that when a girl is in love there's no reasoning with her. If we didn't show that we accepted her man into our life then we risked losing a daughter." The milk crate creaked as he changed his position. "So as a peace offering to our daughter, we gave her the engagement party out here. It was the only thing we could think of to do to show we finally accepted Jordan into our lives."

He paused before he continued. "I can tell you're a

good man. You're a Christian, a true Christian, and I like that about you. I can tell you have feelings for Rainy. I don't know what troubles you're going through, but if you ever want to talk to me or Constance about anything, just let us know. I know you'd never mistreat our Rainy the way that Jordan did."

The barn door opened and a little girl stepped in, wearing faded jeans and an old sweater. Her curly dark hair was pulled into a ponytail, and her mocha-brown eyes were laced with sadness. "Grandpa, Grandma said it's time to eat."

"Hey, Pumpkin." Paul embraced the child in a hug. "Did you meet Mr. Winston? Winston, this is Amber." Winston squeezed her shoulder as they followed her down the path.

"Hi, Mr. Winston." Amber skipped ahead as she ran toward the house.

Paul huffed as they climbed the hill. "Me and my wife don't know what to do about her."

"What do you mean?"

"She's been having trouble at the day care center since her mother left. Mark's been so buried with grief that he hasn't taken the time to spend with his daughter."

Winston glanced at the tyke as she ran into the house, slamming the screen door. "How old is she?"

"She's three. Sometimes she can be quiet, and a little shy. But since the trouble started with her parents, she's been picking fights at school. Plus me and my wife aren't that young anymore. Taking care of a three-year-old child is just wearing us out. I wish Mark would get grief counseling or talk to the pastor…something. I guess it is hard to deal with a cheating mate."

Winston remained silent as they walked into the house. Delicious breakfast scents filled the small kitchen. Constance removed a pan of warm gooey cinnamon rolls from the oven. Bacon fried over the stove and Rainy was scrambling eggs in the skillet. Her jeans hugged her slim frame and her hair was pulled back into a ponytail. He walked to the stove and smiled. "You don't look a day over twenty."

She turned the burner off. "Good morning. Did you sleep well?"

"As well as I could with that storm brewing outside."

Constance removed china plates from the cupboard. "You two need to stop chatting and help me set this table. Winston, the good silverware is in the top drawer."

Minutes later, they were seated at the table. They joined hands, and Paul said grace before they ate the tasty breakfast.

Rainy buttered a biscuit. "Mark's not coming to eat with us?"

Constance glanced at Amber, who continued munching on a cinnamon roll. "No, honey. He's been practically holed up in his room since…well, you know since when. Why don't you take some food up to him? You can even bring Winston with you."

Rainy sprinkled salt over her grits. "I don't know what I can say to make him feel better."

Paul sipped his coffee. "Well, I'm sure you'll think

of something. We've talked to him so much that we've run out of words."

After the meal was finished and the dishes were washed, Rainy fixed a basket of food and Winston walked with her to Mark's house. Winston placed his arm around her waist as he kicked through the blanket of leaves on the walk to the house.

As they approached Mark's house, she turned and faced Winston. "I'm so glad you could come with me."

"I don't mind walking over to Mark's house with you."

She shook her head, causing her dark ponytail to swing in the wind. "I'm not talking about walking to Mark's house. I'm talking about coming home with me. This is a difficult time for me and my family, and…" She paused. His stomach quivered and he fought to keep his mouth from joining hers. "Well, I really needed the support right now."

"I'm glad I could be there for you. I just wish I could spend more time than just the weekend." He gazed at the lush green fields. "It sure is pretty out here in the country."

As he followed her onto the porch, the steps creaked beneath his weight. The boards were faded to a dull shade of mahogany. A rocking chair swung with the cool breeze, making a steady sound against the floorboards.

Rainy rapped against the screen door. "Mark, it's Rainy. Can I come in?" Silence filled the air, so she opened the door and entered.

Winston held his nose as the smell of rotten garbage assailed his nostrils. "My goodness!"

Rainy left the food in the living room, and he followed her into the kitchen. Garbage overflowed onto the dirty kitchen floor and Winston saw a mouse scamper into the corner.

"Ack!" Rainy jumped away from the small creature and Winston took her into his arms.

"Rainy, what happened? It looks like Mark hasn't been here in days!"

"I don't know. My parents were telling me that they talk to Mark every day, but he insisted that he didn't want any visitors. I had no idea it was this bad."

Puddles of dried grease adorned the stove and a carton of milk stood on the counter. Winston continued to gaze around the messy kitchen. "Maybe it's a good thing that Amber isn't staying in this house."

Rainy opened a cupboard. "Amber won't be around here much longer anyway."

"What's that?" Winston knew he had misheard her.

"Amber won't be staying on the farm much longer. Remember, I told you a while ago that my parents had to talk to me about something important?"

Winston nodded. "What did they talk to you about? Was it about Amber?"

Rainy nodded as she pushed her sleeves up and turned the water on. "Amber will be staying with me."

"With you?" He jerked back so hard that he knocked the carton of milk from the counter. As the white liquid spilled to the ground, he quickly mopped it up with a wad of paper towels.

She poured liquid dish detergent into the sink. "Yes.

This is a family crisis and I have to do the best I can to help. Look at this place! My parents are old and they can barely milk those cows and run this farm. Mark's no help. He's not even taking out the trash!" She wrinkled her nose as he threw the soiled napkins into the garbage. "That milk is as curdled as cottage cheese! Ugh, this place is gross!" She threw dishes into the sink.

A loud voice boomed from the top of the stairs. "I told you guys not to come in here!" Heavy footsteps pounded on the floor and seconds later, a man in a faded bathrobe entered the kitchen. His dark scraggly beard and mustache clung to his ashy skin. Dark circles surrounded his mocha-brown eyes.

His eyes suddenly softened, and glistened with unshed tears. "Rainy?" He gazed around his kitchen and bit his lip. He turned away, but Rainy ran to him and held him in her arms.

"I'm so glad to see you again, Mark." She kissed his hair. "You're so thin! You've lost a lot of weight."

"I told Mom and Dad not to come down here. I haven't been feeling right since she left me." He swallowed and looked around his kitchen again. That's when he noticed Winston.

"I'm Winston." They shared a firm handshake.

Mark beckoned them into the living room. The TV and coffee table were coated with dust. Rainy opened the dark curtains and when the sun spilled into the room, Winston noticed Mark's wedding picture still sat on an armoire.

Winston walked toward the door. "Did you two want me to leave?"

"No, please stay, Winston."

Winston plopped into a vacant chair.

Rainy's large brown eyes softened with love as she gazed at her brother. "Mark, you really need to pull yourself together. Do it for Amber's sake. You know how much she loves you."

"I can't take Amber's constant questions now. You know how many questions a three-year-old asks. Well, since her mom left, she has even more questions. Try telling a kid that you don't know where her mother is and you don't know when or if she'll be back." His voice broke on a sob and he turned away.

Rainy squeezed his shoulder. "Mark, you'll get through this, I know you will. Have you been going to church? I'm sure Pastor John would be glad to make time to talk about this."

"Church? Who cares about church, Pastor John or God for that matter!" He cursed and Rainy's eyes widened as she looked at Winston.

Rainy sighed. "Come on, Mark. You used to have such deep faith in God. Going to church might make you feel better."

"I don't know when I'm setting foot in church again. All I ever did to Cindy was be a good and faithful husband. I made a living on this farm and she runs off and leaves me this letter." He removed a crumpled paper from his robe and threw it across the room. "And she tells me she's leaving me for another man, and she doesn't tell me where she's going or how I can contact her! How could she be so cruel to me? How could she abandon her own child like that?" Tears ran down his sunken cheeks and he leaned back into the couch. Everyone was silent and the only sound was the ticking of the grandfather clock in the corner.

Rainy bit her lip before she told him about Amber's recent behavior problems. "Mark, by acting like this, you're abandoning your daughter. You haven't seen her since your wife left you. I'm sure she feels abandoned by both parents."

Mark sighed as he dropped his head in his hands. "You know I love my daughter. I just can't deal with everything right now. I just can't."

She took her brother's palm, caressing the knuckles on his work-roughened hand. "I've come to ask you something."

"What?"

"Well, since Mom and Dad are having a rough time running the farm and taking care of Amber, I've come to ask if it's okay for me to take Amber back with me."

"To Florida?"

She nodded. "Just until you can get yourself together. I love Amber, but I can't raise her. I know she belongs with you since you're her father, but I don't mind keeping her for a while."

She released his hand as he thought about her request. "But if I take her back with me, you're going to have to promise to get some help. You can't stay in a house in this condition. If you keep living like this, the pigs are going to come and join you." A small grin spread over her full lips.

She continued. "And what you might want to do is start milking the cows again. Daddy looks so tired. I'm sure he'd appreciate your help in the barn."

She touched Mark's arm. "As a matter of fact, you've got to help Dad with the milking. I remember how much you used to love getting up early in the morning to milk the cows. Besides, after you spend all that energy milking and feeding the cows, plus the other farm chores, you'll be too tired to think about your wife."

He raised his dark eyebrows as he gazed at Winston and Rainy. "Say, what's up with the two of you?" His eyes suddenly gleamed with mischief.

"Huh?" She placed her hands on her hips as she looked at her brother. "What are you talking about?"

"Well, you haven't brought a man home since that Jordan dude, and I was wondering if you two are serious." He gazed at Winston and Winston wasn't sure what Rainy wanted to reveal to Mark.

She hesitated, glancing at Winston.

Clearing his throat, Winston answered Mark's question. "Rainy is special to me, and I'm glad she let me come home to meet her family."

He cocked his head as he looked at Rainy. "Girl, did you come home to announce another engagement?" She rolled her eyes as she gazed at Winston.

"No!"

A rumbling sound filled the room. "Sorry, folks, that was my empty stomach. It's been a while since I've had some food and I smell one of Mom's country breakfasts right now." He discovered the basket on the couch. He walked into the kitchen and Winston and Rainy followed. Mark opened the cupboard and removed a plate. He then removed silverware from a drawer. After placing the items on the table, he opened the basket.

"I'm glad that you've perked up. But I didn't come home to introduce Winston to the family. Mom and Dad are worried about you, and, frankly, so am I. Is it okay if I take Amber back with me? And will you promise to do what you need to get back on your feet?"

Mark ceased unpacking the basket as he gazed at his little sister. He sighed as he pulled her into his arms. "Yeah, take Amber with you. But this is only temporary. I'll be sure to get her back from you soon. I love my daughter and I don't want her living so far away." As Winston gazed at the moving scene, he felt glad that he'd taken the time to accompany Rainy.

Chapter Twelve

Rainy stared at the busy Miami sidewalk while sipping on her third cup of coffee of the day. She frowned, thinking about how her life had changed since Amber had come into her care.

It was difficult finding time to spend with Winston since she constantly had Amber with her. During Amber's first week in Miami, Winston had generously taken them to the new Disney movie and then to a popular kid-friendly restaurant for dinner. She was glad that Amber seemed to enjoy Winston's company, and she hoped that she made a lot of friends in her new day care center in the newspaper office.

She sighed, continuing to think about her hectic life over the past two weeks. She never thought a three-year-old child could be so much trouble!

She finished her coffee and groaned as she scrutinized the papers littering her desk. She sat in her black leather chair, still staring at the files. "Oh, I guess I need to figure out those spreadsheets." She had been through this three times already. She yawned and stretched. Her phone rang, breaking her concentration.

"This is Rainy."

"Rainy, you need to come down here and get your child," said Beverly, the day care worker.

"Beverly, it's not even five o'clock yet, and the day care is open until six." She pushed her hair away from her face as she rolled her shoulders, trying to ease her tension.

"You don't have to tell me what time it is! I know!" Beverly's thick Jamaican accent carried over the wire. "But you need to get over here and get Amber. She's been misbehaving all day. She even bit a few of the kids! Time out won't work for this one today, so you need to come and talk to her!" She continued to speak, but Rainy didn't have the energy to listen. She sighed as she rang off with Beverly and made the trek to the day care center.

As she opened the door, a multitude of noises flooded her ears. Several children laughed and screamed as they ran around the room. Beverly met her with a reluctant Amber in tow. "You know, both of my day care helpers were sick today, so I'm short-staffed. I don't know what's up with Little Miss, here." She paused, glaring at Amber. "But you need to talk with her. I can't have children biting kids and acting crazy!" She placed her hands on her ample hips. "Amber, you behave yourself tomorrow. We can't have you causing so much ruckus in the day care!"

Amber stared at the floor.

"I'll talk to her, Beverly. Where's your bag?" Amber pointed to her cubbyhole and Rainy retrieved her multicolored backpack.

Rainy used the phone at the day care to call her boss, explaining she had a family emergency. Minutes later, she clutched Amber's hand as they walked into the blaring hot sun. Her heels clattered against the asphalt parking lot. After she had strapped Amber into her car seat, she got into the car and leaned against the steering wheel. Would she even have enough energy to drive home? She swallowed and gazed at Amber, who silently stared out the window. "Amber, you can't act like that in the day care. You know, they had to call me out of work to come and pick you up."

Amber shrugged. "Are you going to send me back to Daddy now?" She glared at Rainy.

"Is that what this is all about?" She exited the car and opened the door to the back seat and sat. She hugged Amber. Deep pain shot through her leg when Amber kicked her with her hard-toed shoes.

Gritting her teeth while enduring the pain, she glared at her niece. "Don't you ever do that to me again, young lady!" She exited the car, slamming the door behind her. She then opened the front door and plopped into the driver's seat, resting her head once on the steering wheel before leaving.

When they arrived home, Amber complained about fatigue, so Rainy sent her to bed. She didn't bother changing her clothes. She sat on her couch and placed her head in her hands. "Lord, help me through this."

After hearing someone knocking at her door, she found the energy to walk to the door and open it. She groaned with relief. "Winston." He still wore his business suit and carried three bags of McDonald's food.

"What happened? You look awful." He entered the house, and after placing the food on the coffee table, he sat beside her on the couch. He ran his finger against the large bruise on her shin. Her panty hose were torn and in spite of the soreness, her skin sizzled from his gentle touch.

"Believe it or not, Amber did it to me."

"Amber? That sweet little girl?"

"You only see her good side! I think she's trying to get away with as much as she can since she's not on the farm. I also think she's still hurting from her mother's abandonment." She leaned her elbows on her knees and tunneled her fingers through her hair. "This has been a rough two weeks. I never knew a child could be so much trouble. I hope she sleeps through the night today, because I need my rest."

He rubbed her shoulder. "Well, I really like Amber, but I did come over here tonight hoping to speak with you alone for a few minutes. I brought McDonald's for all of us." He lifted a bag of food. "I know how much she likes McDonald's."

"Well, she's not getting McDonald's tonight. Not after the way she acted today. She can eat a sandwich or some leftover chicken." She leaned back onto the couch.

"Did you call Mark and your parents about it?"

"No, not yet. I love my niece, but I think I'm ready to send her home and get my life back." She glanced at the food still gracing the table. "I am hungry, though. Why don't we go into the kitchen and eat. I'm thinking you came over here to talk about something."

Minutes later they entered her kitchen. She cringed when she saw the mess left behind. She had not washed dishes in a few days, and they littered the sink. An open carton of milk sat on the table. The scent of sour milk filled the kitchen. "Oh, I forgot to put this away this morning after Amber ate her cereal." She poured the liquid down the sink and threw the carton away. "Sometimes I think I'm losing my mind since Amber came to live with me. I wanted to help my brother out but if this keeps up, *I'm* going to need some help."

He chuckled as he opened a sandwich. After they prayed they enjoyed the simple meal. "Don't be so hard on yourself." He sipped his cola. "I think you two just need to get used to living together." He glanced at her bruised leg. "I hope she doesn't try kicking you like that again."

She sighed, leaning back into her chair. "If she does, I'm sending her back to the dairy farm. I'm so tired that I don't know what to do."

He cleared this throat. "Well, I didn't come over here tonight to talk about Amber. I came to talk about us."

She shrugged. "What about us? I thought we'd agreed to give our relationship a chance before we went to the farm."

"I know. But since you've had Amber, I haven't had any time alone with you. Do you think we could get a baby-sitter so we can go out on a date?"

She smiled as she finished her burger. "I think I could ask Sarah or Rachel to baby-sit on Friday night. I'll let you know what they say."

The next day, Rainy opened the glass door of the restaurant, eagerly scanning the lunch crowd. She hoped Rachel or Sarah were free on Friday night. *I can't wait to spend some time alone with Winston!* The server guided her through the crowded restaurant, and she was surprised to see Rachel had already arrived. She clutched her napkin as she looked through the menu.

Rainy sat beside her friend. "Any of the specials look good today?" She touched Rachel's arm. "What's wrong?" Her hair was tousled and uncombed and her eyes were red-rimmed and tired. She was wearing faded jeans and an old white T-shirt. Rainy gazed at Rachel's hands and saw the nails were bitten down to the skin. "You've been biting your nails! What's the matter and why aren't you dressed for work?"

"I didn't go to work today, or yesterday, either." Her eyes darted around the crowded restaurant. "I hope none of my co-workers are here today. I called in over the past few days. I told my boss I wouldn't be able to come to work."

"Well, if you're sick you shouldn't be here. You don't look so good."

Sighing, she continued to clutch her napkin, pushing Rainy's hand away. "I'm not really sick, but I do have a few problems to deal with. I just can't cope with work right now. My car was repossessed."

Rainy gasped. Before she could respond, Sarah appeared, swinging her small handbag. She placed her purse on the table as she gazed at her friends. "What in the world is wrong with you two? Rainy, you look awful! You've got circles under your eyes, and your hair's pulled back into a hideous-looking ponytail." She paused and gazed at Rachel. "And you look awful, too. You'll never find a husband walking around in public looking like that."

"I'm not desperate to find a man, unlike you," Rachel retorted. She took a deep breath and told Sarah about her recent dilemma.

Sarah's dark eyes softened with concern. "You're kidding? Your car was really repossessed?"

"Yes, and don't ask me how it happened. You get the general idea of how these things work."

"Well, maybe you needed to be attending those financial seminars that Rainy and Winston were doing at the church," suggested Sarah.

"That was for kids. I'm too old for them."

Rainy nodded. "I agree with Sarah. Even though those seminars were for the church youth, they teach young people basic financial skills to use for the rest of their lives. Skills that a lot of African-Americans are never taught. I'll bring over the study plans we used. If you want to talk to either of us about it, feel free to do so."

The server approached the table, placing a basket of

hot rolls and a china dish of butter in the center. "Are you ladies ready to order?"

After they placed their orders, Sarah and Rainy began eating the rolls. Rachel placed her forehead on her palm. "I don't know what I'm going to do. I think I might ask my mom to help me get my car back."

Sarah frowned. "You mean you can pay the amount owed for back payments and get your car back?"

Rachel nodded. "I think so. Oh, I don't know, just thinking about it gives me a headache. I don't want to talk about it anymore."

Sarah nodded as she focused on Rainy. "Okay, we'll drop the subject. So, Rainy, what's been going on with you? You don't look like your life's been easy lately."

Rainy sighed as she pushed her soup aside. Since Amber started living with her, her appetite had lessened considerably. "Well, I was wondering if either of you could do me a favor this Friday night." She told of Amber's recent antics, and then she asked if either would be available so she could go out on a date with Winston.

Rachel folded her arms across her chest. "I think Amber is a dear, and I'm sure her behavior problems will get better. Don't be so discouraged. But I'm just not in the right mindset to baby-sit a child right now, even if it is only for one evening. I'm so depressed about my car and my finances that I don't feel like doing much of anything."

Sarah sipped her water. "I'd watch her for you, but I already have plans for Friday."

"You do? Did you meet another guy through that dating service?" asked Rainy.

"Nope, I'm still dating Carl, the blind man who answered my ad a while ago."

Rainy leaned back into her chair, impressed. "Wow, this is a record for you. You've never been out with someone from the dating service so many times. I never figured you'd find someone who is disabled on the dating ads."

Sarah sighed. "Carl doesn't consider himself disabled. I forget sometimes that he's blind. I'm kind of excited about it. We have so much in common. I don't know what will happen between us, but I can at least see us being good friends. So, Rachel, are you ready to get out of this funk and try to straighten out your life?"

Rachel rolled her eyes. "Please, I'm not in the mood for your lectures right now."

Sarah placed her hands on her slim hips, glaring at Rachel. "You should just heed my advice. You know God would want you to pay back the money you borrowed for your car. It's the right thing to do."

"I know it is. But I don't have enough money to pay everybody. If I did, I wouldn't be in this mess."

Sarah smirked. "Hmph, you wouldn't be in this mess if you'd stop your crazy spending habits. You need to stop buying clothes and jewelry that you don't need!"

Rainy glared at both of her friends. "You two, stop bickering about this. Rachel, you know you can come to me or Winston about your money problems. We might have some suggestions to help you out. Also, there are counselors who help with this sort of thing."

Rainy nibbled on a roll while Sarah continued to preach to Rachel. Closing her eyes, Rainy dreamed about seeing Winston on a real date again. As she chewed, she recalled the last wonderful kiss they had shared.

When she returned home that evening, she put Amber to bed and called Winston. He answered on the first ring.

"Winston, I have bad news. Both Rachel and Sarah can't baby-sit on Friday night." She explained Rachel's financial state and she told him about Sarah's date.

"She's dating a blind man? I always thought Sarah was kind of superficial."

"Hmm. She is very superficial when it comes to looks. I'm not sure what this blind man looks like." After they talked about Sarah, he came up with a solution for their baby-sitting dilemma.

"Well, as far as baby-sitting goes, I think I might have a solution. My aunt and uncle owe me a few favors, so I'll see if they'd be willing to keep Amber on Friday night. I'm almost sure they'd love to have her. Amber will probably have such a good time that she won't be willing to leave when it's time to go."

She grinned, eagerly anticipating the time alone with Winston. "That's a great idea!"

Chapter Thirteen

The following Friday, Winston graced Rainy's door-step, glancing at his watch. He sighed, relieved that he arrived on time. He grinned with anticipation as he rang her doorbell. Amber opened the door. "Hi, Mr. Winston." She grabbed his leg.

"Hi, squirt." He lifted her and kissed her chubby cheek.

"Yuck!" She rubbed her face.

He chuckled as he returned her to the floor. When Rainy strolled out of her bedroom, he whistled. She sported a bright orange sundress that accented her slim yet shapely figure.

"Winston." Her voice was a bare whisper as he took her in his arms. She smelled like spring flowers after a cool rain.

"It's so good to see you again. This'll be our first real date in a long time."

She nodded, her long soft hair tickling his face. Moments later, they deposited Amber at his aunt and uncle's house, where his aunt welcomed them with open arms. Gladys smiled as she embraced Rainy. "So you're the reason my nephew has been so moody lately. It's nice to finally meet you." She released Rainy and quietly complimented Amber on her outfit.

Winston chuckled as he hugged his aunt. "Aunt Gladys, I haven't felt this good in years! You take good care of Amber for us tonight. Hey, where's Uncle Greg?" He glanced around the living room.

"Oh, he had some church stuff to do tonight, but he'll be back later. I've got things to keep Amber busy all evening."

Rainy embraced Amber and kissed her cheek before Winston led her back out to the car. As he drove through the streets of Miami, he found it hard to concentrate on his navigation skills. The night was warm and breezy, so he opened his sunroof.

She crossed her legs. "Where are we going for dinner?"

When he tried to pull a CD from his case, he accidentally brushed her leg. He wondered if Rainy was the woman God intended to be his wife. Being around her was like a ray of sunshine on a cold cloudy day. She haunted his dreams, and he craved her company daily.

"Winston?" He pulled his eyes from the road and stole a glance in her direction. Her mocha-colored eyes were full of excitement as she eagerly gazed at the passing scenery.

"Uh, it's a surprise. You'll see in a few minutes."

Minutes later, they pulled into the parking lot of the restaurant. Jesse's Seafood House was packed; however, for a nominal fee, they had small rooms for diners who wished to eat in private. He held her soft hand as the hostess led them to the private room he'd reserved. Rainy laughed, covering her mouth with her hand. Her eyes sparkled with joy as she gazed around the festive room.

Minutes later, the waiter offered a shrimp cocktail. She brushed the crystal bowl with her long slender fingers. "But we didn't order this."

"I know. We're not ordering anything. I already told them what to serve us tonight. I hope you don't mind." He gazed around the private dining room. Tiny white lights twinkled against the dark walls, reminding him of a Christmas tree. Soft music chimed from the speakers, and a vase of roses decorated the table.

"This is so nice." Her voice was barely above a whisper as she gazed around the room. "But why did you go through so much trouble? This isn't a special occasion."

Before he could respond, the waiter returned with their entrées. After they said a brief prayer, he took both of her hands and massaged her fingers. "You're wrong." He paused. "This *is* a special occasion. This is the first date we've had since we've decided to try this relationship. I'm hoping and praying this'll work out. I just want to tell you that I'm pleased you have faith in me."

"You mean have faith that you won't return to your former drinking problem?"

He shook his head. "No, not former. I'll always be an alcoholic. The urge to drink never really goes away. I've just learned that I need to lean on God. We all have things we need to overcome when we become Christians." He gazed at their hands. His mocha skin blended nicely with her cocoa-brown complexion. "You know, if we ever work everything out, I'm sure we could have some pretty children."

"Winston!" Her brown eyes widened and he squeezed her hand.

"I'm just speaking freely. I think you're a good woman, and in spite of what you think, I believe you're doing a good job caring for Amber. I think we're right for each other, I really do."

He watched her during the entire meal. Her delighted squeals echoed off the velveteen walls as she tried each luscious dish. The soft music played, engulfing them in the sweet notes of the classical songs.

After dinner, he took her to the Black Comedy Theater downtown. When he pulled the tickets from his wallet, she gasped. "That show's been sold out for weeks. How did you get tickets?"

"Well, when you want something bad enough, you find a way to get it. I've got my connections." He confidently placed his arm around her waist and led her into the crowded theater. He enjoyed the show, and he laughed so hard his throat was hurting after the performance.

They stopped at Candace's Creamery for dessert. Teenagers sporting shorts and bathing suits assembled at the round, vanilla-colored tables. Their loud howls of laughter exploded in the small ice-cream shop. She stared at the huge tubs of ice cream lining the refrigerated display cases, brushing her slim fingers against the glass. "Even though I work a few blocks from here, I never thought to come here for ice cream. There are so many flavors, I don't know which to choose." Ice cream in every color of the rainbow was available. After much deliberation, she touched his arm with her now-cold fingers. "Why don't you choose for me?"

He chuckled as he pulled her into his arms, relishing her sweet floral scent. He ordered two banana splits. Since each dish had three scoops of ice cream, he chose six different flavors. The shop was devoid of empty tables, so they carried their treats outside.

The night breeze ruffled the leaves on the palm trees as it whispered through the sky. Her hair lifted in the wind before it settled upon her slim shoulders.

He sighed as he took a second bite. "Man, this is so good!" Nuts, caramel sauce and ice cream mingled on his tongue as he enjoyed each luscious bite. He was so enthralled that he barely heard the automobiles as they passed on the busy Miami street. Sweet notes filled the air, and he recognized the familiar tune playing from the jukebox inside the creamery. "I'm glad those teenagers picked a good song to play." His spoon scraped the bottom of the yellow bowl. "Do you want to dance?"

He stared at her mouth as her tongue swooped her lower lip, catching a drop of melting ice cream. She scraped the bottom of her bowl as she spooned the last bite into her mouth.

She licked her lips and frowned as she glanced at her watch. "Look how late it is. I don't think we have time to dance. We'd better get back. We promised your aunt we wouldn't stay out too late."

He huffed as he held her hand while walking to his car. Warm, glowing feelings covered his entire being. The buildings that rose against the midnight black sky, the palm tree leaves as they fluttered in the wind, the raucous laughter in the creamery, the taste of chocolate, vanilla and bananas…he would remember all of this for as long as he lived. Most of all he would remember how pretty Rainy looked in her tangerine dress. Her brow furrowed with worry as she thought about her beloved niece. *Lord, I hope she is worried and concerned about me like that…eventually. Oh, please, Lord, please make it happen!*

Before he opened her door, he pulled her into his arms. He held her so tight that he could feel her ribs beneath her cotton dress.

"What's wrong?" Her dark eyes were laced with concern as he touched her cheek.

I love you, that's what's wrong with me. He caressed her flat stomach and held her slender arm. "You've lost weight. I hope you're taking care of yourself."

"Since we arrived at the creamery, you've been acting strange. Maybe they put something in that ice cream."

She entered the car and he strolled to the driver's side. Driving to his aunt Gladys's house, he drove slowly, savoring each minute of this wonderful evening. He opened his sunroof again, glancing at the stars at every stoplight. He glimpsed at Rainy as she ran her fingers through her long dark hair. He watched her chew her lower lip as she anxiously checked her watch. Their journey finally came to a close as he pulled into the driveway, the car crunching pebbles of gravel. He pulled her hand into his as they entered the house.

Aunt Gladys pushed her glasses on her nose as she looked up from her needlepoint. "My, don't you two look like you had a good time. Winston, I'm glad to see you smiling so much."

Rainy squeezed his hand. "How's Amber?"

Gladys placed her needlepoint into a tan wicker basket. "The Little Miss is fast asleep. I put her in the spare bedroom."

The rich scent of chocolate filled the living room. He sniffed as he buried his hand in his pocket. "It sure smells good in here. Don't tell me you were showing Amber your secret brownie recipe." He turned to Rainy. "I ate so many of those once that I got sick."

Heavy footsteps pounded on the hardwood floor. Uncle Greg stepped into the room, embracing Rainy in his large arms. "I'm so glad to finally meet you, young lady." Rainy returned his hug.

"It's nice to meet you, too. I've heard some nice things about you."

When he released her, he turned to Winston. "Why

don't you come back into my office? I just got some new additions to my stamp collection."

Winston rolled his eyes. "Uncle Greg, I'd love to see them, but Rainy has to take Amber home."

Gladys folded her arms. "You two don't need to worry about that! That child's sleeping so hard that it won't matter what time you take her home. Go on back there and look at your uncle's collection."

Winston sighed and squeezed Rainy's hand before he followed his uncle out of the room.

Rainy smiled at Winston's aunt. "I really appreciate your keeping Amber for us tonight. Winston had a special night planned."

Gladys served coffee in the living room. Rainy sniffed the fragrant brew before she took a sip. "I hope I'll be able to sleep tonight. It's after twelve o'clock, and I've had a full dinner, ice cream for dessert, and now this coffee."

"Oh, I'm sure you'll be okay. Both of you deserved a night of romance."

Gladys sipped her coffee and offered Rainy a brownie. She declined as she continued to enjoy her drink.

"It was no trouble at all keeping Amber. I know how hard it can be to take care of a young one. So you and Winston had a good time?"

She nodded. "We sure did. I was so surprised that he planned such a special evening."

"I can tell you're special to him. You're a good Christian woman and that's what he needs. You know, I was so touched when he told me about his decision to live his life according to God's laws. That was one good thing that came out of his twin sister's death."

Rainy wrinkled her brow as she placed her cup back onto the china saucer. "I'm afraid I don't understand."

"Oh, you know what I mean." Gladys's eyes softened with respect. "I know his sister's death hit him pretty hard. It was hard on the whole family. But at least Winston cleaned his life up."

"Cleaned his life up?"

"Why, yes. I'm sure he told you he got baptized shortly after his sister's death. He hasn't had a drink since. His parents raised him in the church, and he's always believed in God, but he never took the big step and got baptized until she died." She paused and stared at the picture of Jesus adorning her wall, her voice wavering as she continued. "He'd turned to drinking again while she had breast cancer, and we were all so worried about him. But we're proud of the way he's gotten his act together. I'm sure you've realized just how deep his faith has become since she died."

Rainy sighed as she stared at the wall. Disbelief, shock and apprehension coursed through her veins as she digested this piece of news. How deep could Winston's faith be if he was baptized so recently? Why hadn't he mentioned this before?

"Rainy, you're frowning. Is something wrong?"

She shook her head. "Are you sure Amber's okay? I wonder how much longer Winston will be." She glanced at her watch. "I want to get Amber to bed."

"Oh, let me go and see what's taking them so long. You know how talkative some men can be when they get together. My husband babbles on forever about his stamp collection." She left the room, her light steps fading down the darkened hallway.

Rainy squeezed her hands as she waited for Winston to return. Why hadn't he told her about this? Minutes later, he walked into the living room, carrying the slumbering Amber in his arms. Gladys and Greg followed close behind.

Rainy clenched her teeth, wondering how she would make the trip home and not lose her reserve. She said a brief farewell to Gladys and Greg, while still trying to digest this newfound information.

Winston pulled onto the highway as Amber's soft snores filled the silent car. "Why are you so quiet?"

"I'll tell you once we're home and we've put Amber to bed." She twisted the leather strap on her purse so hard it almost snapped.

When they arrived at her house, Winston deposited Amber into her room. Rainy removed Amber's socks and shoes and changed her into her pajamas. Minutes later, they returned to the living room.

Winston shoved his hands into his pockets. "Did my aunt scare you away?"

"Something like that," she murmured.

His smile faded as he touched her face. "What's wrong? What happened?"

"Why didn't you tell me you'd just been baptized fairly recently?"

He dropped his hand and stepped away. "Fairly recently?"

She nodded. "You were an alcoholic when your sister had cancer. You didn't dedicate your life to Christ until she died. Yet you led me to believe you'd been saved a long time ago."

"Whoa, back up a minute." He sat on the couch. "I never really told you when I was baptized."

She sighed as she sat down. "Well, when you told me about your battle with alcoholism that night on the cruise, you led me to believe you were saved when you admitted you had a problem and you started going back to church. I thought you ended your battle with alcoholism sometime after college, after you broke up with your girlfriend."

"I tried to tell you tonight, the battle with alcoholism never ends. It'll always be there. And, frankly, I'm puzzled about your reaction to my aunt's news. I know I didn't tell you when I'd been baptized while we were on the cruise, but the only thing that's important is that I did declare Christ as my Lord and Savior and I'm saved now. Why should it matter if I did it ten days ago or ten years ago? I did it and in the Lord's eyes that's good enough."

She sighed as she rested her forehead into her hand. "It *does* matter. I've noticed that new converts sometimes revert back to their old ways. I'm just worried about your turning toward alcohol for solace again."

"I haven't had a drink since I was baptized. I was baptized a week after my sister died. When Pam died,

I didn't know what to do to deal with the grief. I'd never lost someone who was so close to me before."

His voice wavered as he continued. "When Pam was sick on chemotherapy, I wished I could take some of that pain away from her. She was hospitalized near the end of her life, and when I visited her, she told me how her faith in Christ was seeing her through this ordeal. I'd always admired my sister's deep faith, and I often wondered if I had it in me to follow her example. She told me if she died, she wanted to make sure she left her Bible with someone who would take care of it."

His jaw tensed as he continued his story, and his eyes glistened with unshed tears. "She told me to give the Lord a chance and see what I thought. So after her death, I decided to give Him a chance. So far, I'm glad that I have. I'm finding it hard to do God's will all the time, but I think I'm a better person for making such a big step in my life."

She moved to the couch and touched his arm. "I'm glad you shared this with me. I know we agreed not to keep secrets from each other and I need to tell you how I'm feeling." She paused. "I still question your faith. I don't mean this to be an attack against you personally, but you dedicated your life to Jesus after your sister's death. You were still hurting, and you wanted to do something that Pam wanted you to do. I still wonder if you might have been baptized just to please her, not because you sincerely wanted to."

"I'm not a child, and I have a mind of my own. Pam might have pushed me in the right direction, but I would have eventually taken the right road to Jesus."

"This is just so much information that I need to think about it."

"Do you mean this changes things between us? You're holding my date of baptism against me? Rainy, that hurts."

She continued to rest her hand on his shoulder. "I don't mean to hurt you. But you can't question my decision. You got baptized to please your sister's wishes, just as Jordan pretended to be a Christian to please me. What would happen if you were to have another tragedy? Would you turn to the bottle, or would you lean on Jesus?"

His intake of breath was so hard, he sounded physically injured. "I think it's time for me to leave now. I don't want to say anything that I'll regret. Perhaps we can continue this discussion later." He closed the door and she heard him start his engine before driving away.

Tears dampened her face upon his exit. "Lord, what will I do now? Is Winston really serious about his faith in You, or is this just something he's doing to please the wishes of his sister? Have I offended him by implying he got baptized for the wrong reasons? Have I offended You, dear Lord, by questioning his faith, which could be just as strong as that of an old and seasoned Christian?" Her tears continued to run freely, and she wondered if they would ever stop.

His confession was confusing. Why had he not told her this while they were on the cruise? Was he trying to hide this fact about his Christianity? Was she making an issue out of nothing?

When she went to bed that night, she curled into a ball beneath her blue comforter. Her salty tears continued to fall as she prayed herself to sleep.

Rainy moved through the next few days as if in a trance. She dropped Amber off at day care before she went to work each morning. The only thing she was pleased about was that Amber's behavior problems seemed to diminish. Every evening, she made a new habit of sitting with Amber before bed, reading one of the Bible stories used in her church's Sunday school primer.

The following Saturday, she finally found some time to relax in spite of the bad weather. Rain pounded on the roof as she flipped through the latest issue of *Essence* magazine. Thunder clapped, and she barely paid attention to the words printed on the page. The television was tuned to a popular movie channel, but she couldn't concentrate on the show.

Her living room was littered with crayons, coloring books and toys. She smiled, relishing the silent house. *I'm so glad Amber is at Sister Mary's grandchild's birthday party!*

She dropped the magazine on the floor and piled her pillows on the couch. She lay back and closed her eyes.

She missed Winston.

Their recent separation had been draining on her. His face popped into her mind at the most inopportune times. She was grateful that she was keeping Amber, because the diversion helped with her grief. She sighed as she pressed her hand against her head. Should she call him and apologize?

The loud rap at the door resounded in the room. Her eyes fluttered open, and she shuffled to the door. "Sarah!"

Sarah breezed into the living room, her companion right behind her. Large drops of rain splattered the carpet. Sarah giggled, closing her umbrella. The stranger gracing Sarah's arm was about six feet tall and as bulky as a football player. He wore a pair of dark shades, and he carried a folded red-tipped white cane in his hand.

Rainy swallowed and stared. She finally managed to greet her surprise guests. Sarah's dark skin glowed, and she grinned as she carefully stepped around the toys on the floor and led her friend to the couch. The subtle floral scent of her perfume pleasantly filled the room.

"Me and Carl were going to the outdoor festival but it was rained out. Since we were in the neighborhood, I thought we'd stop by and say hello. Carl, this is my friend, Rainy."

Rainy shook his hand and he turned his sightless eyes toward her. "I'm glad to finally meet you, Rainy. Sarah's always talking about you." His grin produced two dimples on his cheeks.

"Where's Amber?" Sarah glanced around the empty house. She told her about the birthday party Amber was attending.

"Oh, well, I'm kind of sorry we stopped by then. You don't get much free time to yourself nowadays, so I'm sure you're enjoying this time alone." Suddenly, Sarah's face was a few inches from hers. "Rainy, what's wrong?"

"It's Winston." She glanced at Carl, unsure of how to proceed.

"Carl, me and Rainy are going into her bedroom to talk."

Rainy hesitated, staring at Carl. "I don't want to interrupt your date."

Carl grinned. "I'll be all right. Where's your remote? The game's on and I wanted to watch it. By the way, do you have anything to drink?"

She entered her kitchen and returned minutes later with a cola and a bag of chips for Carl. She changed the channel to his desired station and led Sarah into her bedroom.

"Rainy, this room looks awful!"

Rainy gave her room a thorough scrutiny. Her bed was mussed, and a vase of dead flowers rested on her dresser. "You know, Amber's been draining all my energy. She won't sleep on the pullout couch in the living room. She always climbs in bed with me, claiming she's scared. Then she tosses and turns all night. I love her, but I don't know how long it's going to take me to adjust to this life."

"So that's why you look so drained? Amber's been keeping you up?" Sarah touched her arm as they sat on the bed.

Rainy rested her forehead on her hand. "No, not really. Something terrible happened last week, and I feel so ashamed that I didn't want to tell you and Rachel."

"Oh? What happened?"

She finally found the courage to tell her about her confrontation with Winston. When she was finished, she felt tears streaming down her cheeks. Sarah gave her a tissue and she wiped her eyes and blew her nose. "Do you think I was wrong?"

"Hmph, I'm surprised you would even ask me that. I can tell by your reaction that you know your actions were wrong." There was a chill to Sarah's voice that was not softened by Rainy's tears.

Rainy toyed with the fringe of her blue silk comforter. "But don't you see? How can I trust that Winston is really a Christian? He's only doing this in memory of his deceased sister, not because he feels it in his heart."

"Weren't you listening to the reverend at church last Sunday?"

She tried to reach into the inner recesses of her cluttered brain. She vaguely recalled Amber being restless during the service, and they had to make several trips to the rest room. "You know how Amber was acting up last Sunday."

"Well, the subject was baptism. And he read Luke chapter three, verse three. When you're baptized, you're repenting for the remission of sins. Winston used to be an alcoholic. I've gotten to know him since you guys started working together in the church. I don't think he's had a drink since his sister died. If he told you this, then I'd believe him. Winston is no saint, but he's not a liar."

Thunder rolled through the sky and the rain continued to pelt against the window. Fatigue settled into her bones, and Rainy longed to settle into the comforter and fall asleep. "I'm not doubting that."

"Then what's the problem?" Sarah threw her hands up in the air. "Who cares if his sister's death made him see the light? It doesn't matter *why* he got baptized, as long as he is trying to live his life according to God's rules the best that he can. That's all God asks of us. You know we're all sinners." Her voice was tinged with impatience.

"I don't know. There's just so much I have to sort through. I've already been burned once by false Christianity."

"Oh, so that's what this is all about? You're still upset about being duped by Jordan. Well, Jordan is a liar, and you shouldn't trust him. But you shouldn't punish Winston for Jordan's mistake. Rainy, that's just plain wrong."

"But don't you see? My experience with Jordan made me learn my lesson. I shouldn't trust men so easily."

Sarah stood and paced around the messy room. "Hmm. Trust? As far as I can remember, trust should be earned, and Winston has earned your trust, don't you think? He's never lied to you. He told you about his battle with alcoholism, and his apprehensions about turning back to the bottle for solace. I think you can trust Winston." She sat on the bed and took Rainy's hand. "You're one of my best friends, and I'd hate to see you lose out on a good man just because you don't see things as they are." She smiled and squeezed her hand.

Sarah tilted her head toward the living room. "Speaking of seeing…what do you think about Carl?" The noise from the TV sports game blared into the room. "He's kind of cute, isn't he?"

Rainy smiled, pleased with the diversion in conversation. "Yes. He talks like a sighted person, though. Watching a game? He can't see."

Sarah shrugged. "I know. But he still enjoys the same things that sighted people do. He told me that through sound and touch, he sees things in his mind, and that's good enough for him. He also said that was God's unique way of allowing him to see."

Sarah giggled and hugged herself.

"I'm glad that you're so happy." Rainy squeezed her hand. "Do you think that he's the one? Maybe you guys could get married someday."

"Whoa, hold on. We've only been going out for a few months, so it's hard to tell if he's the one. But I like him. He's stable, too. He's got a good job with the government and he has his own house."

"You've been to his house?"

Sarah nodded, causing her earrings to clatter. "Yep. It's really cool. He has this special computer with an adaptive braille pad. He can read anything on the computer screen because it transposes into braille." Warmth and enthusiasm tinged her voice.

"Well, I must say, it's been years since I've seen you so excited over a man. I hope he makes you happy." She

hoped Sarah could find love and happiness, because
Rainy didn't know if love would ever figure into
her own life.

Chapter Fourteen

The next day, Rainy entered Friendship Community Church, sighing with relief when they made it in time. Rachel and Sarah approached, hugging Rainy and Amber.

Amber fingered her freshly starched and pressed white dress. "Do you like my dress, Miss Rachel and Miss Sarah?" Her large brown eyes were eager for compliments.

Sarah kissed Amber's chubby cheek. "You look fine, sweet pea. Let me take you down to Sunday school." Rainy squeezed Sarah's shoulder as she led Amber away.

Rachel pulled Rainy into a secluded corner of the foyer. People assembled in clumps as their voices filled the wide space. "Did you see Winston? I didn't realize he was coming to church today. Is he thinking about becoming a member? Me and Sarah were just talking to him a few minutes ago, and he didn't look so good."

Her heart thumped as she gazed at the sea of brown faces cluttering the foyer. She swallowed as she clutched Rachel's hand. "Where is he?"

Rachel adjusted her decorative yellow hat. "He already went into the sanctuary. But, girl, let me tell you, he looked so worn and haggard! You didn't tell us he's growing a beard."

She forced herself to relax. Rachel touched her shoulder. "Hey, what's wrong? Did you two have another argument?"

She nodded so hard, her hair almost escaped from the bun at the nape of her neck. "I don't want to discuss it right now, but we had a terrible disagreement about a week ago."

Rachel folded her arms in front of her full chest. "I'm confident you two will work this out. You both have a deep faith in God, and that's all you need."

Rainy chewed on her lower lip as she glanced into the crowded sanctuary. Perhaps she could find a seat in the back, far away from Winston. Thunderous music spilled from the sanctuary as the choir broke into song. Rachel grabbed her hand. "Come on, let's go find ourselves a seat! I'm sure Sarah will find us soon enough." Rainy followed Rachel into the sanctuary and they found a seat near the center of the church. She searched the aisles, breathing a sigh of relief when she didn't spot Winston. Perhaps he'd changed his mind and gone home or decided to leave and worship at his own church.

As the choir sang sweet songs, worshiping the Lord,

Rainy closed her eyes, issuing a silent prayer to God. As the service continued and the sermon was presented, she found her mind wandering on other things. Reverend Marshall was issuing his invitation for people to step forward when an usher slid a cream-colored envelope into her hand. Her heart pounded as she ripped it open. She sighed with relief when she discovered it was from Karen Marshall, Reverend Marshall's wife. It read: I'd like to see you after service. Please meet me in my husband's office after the benediction, if possible.

Moments later, Rainy strolled into Reverend Marshall's office. She walked around his quarters, checking her watch, feeling relieved that Rachel and Sarah agreed to take Amber to the pancake house for breakfast, where she would meet them when she was finished with the reverend.

She touched a volume of a set of religious encyclopedias. Dust coated her finger and she rubbed it into her hands.

High heels clattered on the hardwood floor. Karen Marshall entered her husband's office, sporting a yellow sheath dress. She resembled a high-energy canary as she hurried about the room, checking stacks of papers. "Oh, he's not here yet!" She clutched her hands and checked her watch. She ran her fingers through her short gray hair.

"Mrs. Marshall, who's not here yet? I got the message that you wanted to see me after service." Rainy placed her small black leather purse on the desk.

Karen waved in her direction. "Oh, I'm so glad you made it. I know Winston is here today. I called him last night and he promised me he'd come!"

Her heart seemed to drop ten stories. Winston was coming here, into Reverend Marshall's office? Questions jumped through her mind as fast as popping kernels of corn. She opened her mouth, hoping to ask at least one question. Before she could utter a sound, Winston stepped into the office.

It had been a little over a week since their disagreement, and he looked just as haggard as Rachel described. She fought to resist the urge to hold his hand and kiss his cheek. His sadness cut through her like a knife. She'd hurt him, and there was nothing she could do about it.

Karen Marshall fluttered about the office before she closed the door. "Oh, Winston, I'm so glad you're here!" She pushed him into one of the thick leather chairs and motioned for Rainy to sit. "Rainy, I would have called you last night, but I'm so absentminded that I lost your phone number. Sending you a note during service seemed to be the best way to get you here afterward." She pulled a pair of glasses from the desk and placed them on her thin nose. Pulling a stack of papers toward her, she faced both of them. Pursing her lips, she scanned through the papers. "I have here a copy of the script for the Christmas pageant. I'm sure my husband spoke to you two about leading this ministry."

Winston cleared his throat. Rainy closed her eyes as she enjoyed the sweet tangy scent of his cologne. "Mrs.

Marshall!" His deep voice blended with her shaky tone. He looked at her, his hazel eyes full of sorrow. "I'm sorry. You go first."

She squeezed the wooden chair arm. "Mrs. Marshall, Winston and I never gave Reverend Marshall a response about the pageant." She paused, praying for her thundering heart to slow down.

Winston cleared his throat again. "Mrs. Marshall, we won't be able to lead the children's ministry. I'm sorry if we misled Reverend Marshall into thinking otherwise."

Karen's small birdlike mouth pursed as she removed her glasses. "My goodness! Why not? Is it because you're not a member of the church, Winston? Are you uncomfortable getting more involved with this church when you have your own church?"

He shook his head. "No, it's nothing like that. I don't have a problem in doing God's calling in this church."

Mrs. Marshall shook her head. "I don't understand."

Rainy started sniffling. She quickly pulled a tissue from the box and blew her nose. She turned away, not wanting to expose her suddenly damp eyes.

"My goodness, Rainy, what on earth is the matter?" Mrs. Marshall's voice softened as she approached Rainy.

Winston's chair scraped against the floor as he stood. "Mrs. Marshall, could you leave us alone for a minute?"

Rainy stood, hoping her legs could withstand her weight. "No, don't leave us alone. I really need to get going."

Warmth and sincerity shined from Karen Marshall's dark eyes as she gazed at the two parishioners. "I think I understand now. How about I leave you two here for a while? Rainy, nobody is forcing you to stay, but just remember you need to have faith in Jesus to work through your problems." She paused as she walked to the door. "That advice goes to both of you."

Rainy sighed as she turned away from Winston. "I had no idea you'd be here today." She swallowed and walked to the window. Bright sunlight spilled into the room, illuminating tiny dust motes as they danced in the air.

He joined her at the window, placing his hand on her shoulder. "You not only need to have faith in Jesus, but you need to have faith in me. You need to give me…give *us* a chance. Our faith in God is already the most solid foundation for a relationship."

Rainy squeezed her eyes shut. This was so hard! She'd missed Winston so much over the past week. Was she being foolish? Being with Amber helped to dull the ache that carved her heart. However, she knew she needed more than the love of a child to see her through this. "I still need some more time to think about this."

He sighed. "Well, you can think about it if you want to. But don't think about it too long. I can't wait forever." The soft warmth from his hand evaporated and his heavy footsteps sounded on the wooden floor as he exited the room.

Rainy continued to think about her unexpected encounter with Winston over the next few days. He plagued her thoughts and dreams, and she constantly prayed for the courage to do the right thing.

She was still thinking about Winston when she returned home from work in the middle of the week, exhausted. She changed her clothes and sat on the couch and rested for a few minutes before Amber declared she wanted dinner. She sighed as she walked into the kitchen to give her the evening meal. As she scooped leftovers onto a plate, she wondered how much longer she could care for her beloved niece. She knew that once Amber was back home, she would miss her like crazy, but on the other hand, she wanted her freedom and her single life back. As she placed the plate in the microwave and pressed the button, her phone rang.

"Hello."

Her brother's voice carried over the wire, deep and strong, with just a twinge of happiness. "Sister dear, how is everything?"

"Mark?" She clutched the phone, still in disbelief that her brother could sound so ecstatic.

"The one and only. I was wondering if you were ready to give Amber back now?" As if on cue, Amber left the table and pulled Rainy's blue jeans with her small hands.

"Is that Daddy? Can I talk to him?" Rainy gave her the phone as she finished dinner. Minutes later, she took the phone back from Amber. She hurriedly made preparations with Mark to return his daughter.

"You sound much better." She sat at the table as Amber ate her dinner.

"Yeah, I've been to see Pastor John a few times, and I've started going to church again." He paused and the heavy silence carried over the wire. "I've heard from Cindy."

"She called you?"

"Yeah. She's back in town and she wants to see Amber. I didn't mention it to Amber since I don't want her getting her hopes up about seeing her mom again."

Rainy sighed as she twisted the phone cord. "I can understand that."

"So, how's Amber been acting?"

She gazed fondly at her niece as she continued enjoying her dinner. "Sometimes good, and sometimes not so good. You know how it goes with children." Questions about Cindy's return swirled through her mind, but she didn't want to ask in front of Amber, and she figured she'd get better answers once she saw him in person again.

She rang off with Mark after agreeing to the arrangements to return Amber. Amber scraped the plate with her fork. "Aren't you going to eat, Aunt Rainy?"

Rainy shook her head as she sat in the chair. Perhaps she'd find the energy to eat dinner later. Since she'd broken up with Winston, she'd found her appetite had almost diminished. She felt sad, guilty and tired. The only bright spots in her days were her job and Amber.

When Rainy told Amber the good news, she jumped from her seat. "Yeah! I'm gonna see my daddy." To celebrate, Rainy took Amber out for a sundae at Candace's Creamery.

Hours later, Rainy sat alone, thinking about her mistake. She was so embarrassed that she couldn't bring herself to apologize to Winston. After Amber was in bed, she wrote him a letter, asking forgiveness, and seeking the possibility of meeting next week to discuss the matter. She still felt scared and afraid, but hopefully she would learn to trust Winston and get over the experience she'd had with Jordan.

She mailed the letter the day before she boarded a plane to return Amber to Mark. She hoped when she returned that Winston would welcome her back into his life with open arms. If he didn't, she knew that she couldn't really blame him. She'd already caused enough hurt and pain with her actions and she knew that Winston had had enough trouble and heartache over the past year to last him a lifetime.

Winston pulled into his driveway, exhausted from his game of basketball. He found that playing the sport, as well as running numerous laps on South Beach, helped to exhaust him to the point that he didn't think about Rainy so much.

Sweat poured down his skin as he clutched his basketball under his arm. As he pulled the mail from his box, the wind blew and rain started pouring from the sky. He dropped a letter, and before he could retrieve it, it blew away. "Probably a bill," he muttered as he walked toward his home. He saw the letter land behind a bush, and the return address caught his eyes. "It's from Rainy," he breathed. He dumped the rest of his mail in the foyer as the rain continued to pour from the sky.

The envelope and letter were drenched, but he did manage to decipher from the wet, mottled script that Rainy wanted to speak with him. He quickly dialed her number and was disappointed to get her answering machine. He recalled her late nights at the office so he called her work phone number and heard her voice mail state that she would be out of the office for part of the following week.

He slammed the phone down and paced his living room. It continued to rain, and he barely listened to the droplets of water as he tried to figure out a plan of strategy. He had to see Rainy and he didn't want to wait for her to return from wherever she was. Was she out of town, or was she merely taking a few days off? Was she having more problems with Amber? These questions plagued his brain as he paced his living room floor.

He finally returned to his car and drove to her house. The thunderstorm made his driving more troublesome, and he turned his windshield wipers on. About a half hour later, he pulled into Rainy's driveway and was disappointed to see that her car was nowhere in sight. "Where could she be?" he muttered.

He recalled Sarah's address. Minutes later he pulled into Sarah's driveway. Lights winked from the windows amid the torrid rain. He ran to her door and pounded on it. Minutes later, she opened it. "Winston!" He quickly strolled into the house and stopped as soon as he saw the chunky man with dark glasses sitting in her living room. A decorated cake with candles sat on the coffee table and cups of steaming coffee filled the air with their aromatic scent. Sarah was decked out in a yellow dress and her face was made up. She glared at him, seemingly disappointed that her date had been interrupted. "Sarah, who is it?" The man's deep voice filled the room as he stood.

"It's okay, Carl, it's just Winston, Rainy's friend. Carl, this is Winston—Winston, I'd like you to meet Carl." She introduced them as she guided Carl's hand toward Winston's. That's when he realized the man was blind. A red-tipped white cane stood in the corner. They shared a firm handshake before Carl returned to his seat. Sarah led Winston into the kitchen. He noticed two dirty plates at the table and a set of matches on the counter.

"Okay, Winston, this had better be good. I was just about to light the candles on Carl's birthday cake." She glared, placing her hands over her lean hips.

"I didn't mean to interrupt your date, but this is an emergency. Where's Rainy?"

"Hmm. I don't know if I should tell you that. Do you know if she wants to talk to you?" She pulled a cake knife from the drawer and lifted the matches from the counter.

He sighed. "Of course she wants to talk to me. That's why I'm here." He explained how her letter had gotten wet in the rain. "I couldn't make out all the words, but I know she wants to meet with me sometime next week."

"Well, I know you wouldn't lie about something like this." She told him that Rainy had returned to her parents' dairy farm to return Amber. "Mark wanted to pick her up, but he couldn't leave the farm chores for the weekend."

"Thank you." He kissed her cheek, said goodbye to Carl and ran out of the house. The rain continued to fall, but the thunder and lightning had stopped. When he returned home, he called his travel agent and booked a flight for the following day. Rainy Jackson was going to be getting a surprise visit tomorrow. He just hoped and prayed her letter had stated that they should reconcile and try to renew their relationship.

The scent of cow dung and hay filled the cool autumn air as Rainy walked to the secluded brook on her parents' dairy farm. Cows mooed in the distance, eagerly awaiting the evening milking. She sat on a rock and snuggled beneath her jacket.

She smiled as she fondly recalled Amber's reunion with Mark. He'd cried tears of joy as he clutched his beloved daughter. She hoped and prayed everything worked out for the small family. Cindy, Amber's mother, had returned for a brief period of time. She'd spent a few hours with Amber, and had arranged to visit her regularly with Mark. Rainy still had unexplained questions about Cindy's sudden reappearance, and she wondered if she was still with the man she'd had an affair with. She questioned where Cindy was staying and found that she was staying in town with a relative.

She sighed as the cool evening air blew through the trees. She still ached to speak to Winston, but she just couldn't find the courage to call him. She almost dialed his number three times, but after punching in a few of the digits, she'd hung up the phone in frustration. She knew he must have received her letter by now, and when she checked her home and work numbers, she didn't have any messages from him. "Lord, does this mean I've messed things up pretty badly? Does Winston not want to be a part of my life any longer?" She asked aloud.

"I've wanted to be a part of your life, Rainy, ever since we first met on the cruise." Winston's deep voice carried over the wind. She gazed behind her. Was she dreaming?

Winston walked toward her, and he looked as fine as ever! His dark jeans hugged his lean hips and his jacket covered his broad shoulders. "Winston, what are you doing here?" She moistened her dry lips as she gazed at the man that she loved.

"I'm here to see you."

"But, how did you find me?"

He sat beside her on the rock and took her hand. As he caressed her fingers, sparks of warmth flowed through her arm.

"I paid Sarah a surprise visit and she told me I'd find you here." He pensively gazed at the green pastures and the sparkling brook.

"You flew down here to see me?" She cocked her head and gave him a confused look. "Why? I was going to be home next week. Didn't Sarah tell you that?"

"Yes, she told me. But I wanted to see you in person, and I didn't want to wait until you got back to talk to you."

"Oh." She looked toward the brook, and the pine trees dotting the land. "I'm surprised you're here. In light of the way I've been treating you."

"Rainy..." She placed her fingers over his full lips.

"Let me finish," she calmly demanded. She sighed as the breeze blew through her hair, lifting the strands off her neck. "It was wrong of me to question your reasons for your baptism. As long as people come to Him, God doesn't care about the reasons and neither do I. You're living your life as a Christian, and I'm sure your sister's death shook you up pretty much. It was wrong of me to misjudge you like that and I'm sorry."

"Oh, Rainy. I know you're sorry. I just want us to try to work through this. I know it's hard to believe I've turned my life around completely since Pam's death, but I have improved the best that I can."

He paused as he caressed her shoulder. "You look too thin. You haven't been eating, have you?"

She gazed into his hazel-brown eyes. "No, I've been too upset to eat."

She was silent as she thought about his words. Could she trust him? Could she allow the anger and hurt to evaporate? Would he return to alcohol when he had a crisis?

He cleared his throat. "I can tell you're hesitant about this relationship. Did you need to think about it over the weekend? I won't bother you until you're ready to give me an answer." When she gazed into his hazel eyes, she noticed they glistened with tears. She touched his cheek, brushing his razor stubble.

Her voice wavered as she spoke. "No, I won't have to think about it this weekend. I can tell you right now."

He patiently waited until she spoke.

"My answer is yes, Winston." She pulled him into her arms and they shared a long hug.

Chapter Fifteen

Rainy turned her computer off and packed her briefcase. A soft knock sounded on her door. "Come in."

Caroline, her new office assistant, stepped into the room. "Are you about ready to leave, Rainy?" Her steno pad was open and she clutched a gold pen.

"Yes, it's about that time, Caroline." She smiled as she relished Caroline's cool professional manner. Her dark suit was freshly pressed and her black hair was pulled back into a bun. Round, dark-framed glasses rested upon her nose.

Caroline waved the steno pad in the air. "Just wanted to remind you to get here early tomorrow morning. You have a breakfast meeting with the auditors at eight o'clock." Rainy praised God for allowing her to find a competent assistant. She never would have remembered the meeting tomorrow without her.

"Thanks, Caroline. Why don't you go home yourself now?"

Caroline nodded. "I will as soon as I finish typing up those letters."

Rainy yawned as she left her office and walked downstairs. The past six months had been hectic. She was saddened that she finally had to have Linda fired. After several warnings, as well as office etiquette training seminars, she still had not improved her office manner. Her behavior had gotten worse, so she had to be removed from the job. Rainy had thought and prayed about it for weeks before she finally took the final step.

As she continued through the building, she said goodbye to several of her co-workers. She stopped as she approached the day care center. Children shrieked, and she heard cries coming from the room. A pang of sadness sliced through her as she thought about her niece, Amber. It had been six months since she'd kept her temporarily, and she still missed her like crazy. As a result of the temporary status of motherhood, she'd taken it upon herself to call Amber every night, just to say hello and to see how she was doing.

"I think about that girl every day," she mumbled as she exited the building. She listlessly gazed at the sidewalk as she walked to her car.

"Winston," she breathed. He leaned against her car, clutching a dozen red roses. She glided toward him and he held her in his arms, crushing the flowers.

He pressed his lips to her ear. "Hi, sweetheart." She reluctantly ended their embrace.

"Why are you here? We didn't have a date set for tonight."

"I wanted to see you, and I didn't want to wait until our next date. Is that a crime, young lady?"

She smiled as she touched his razor-stubbed cheek. "No, as a matter of fact, I'm glad to see you." He lifted the floral bouquet into her arms. She sniffed the sweet fragrance. Several of her co-workers walked by and chuckled. "Are you sure you don't have a reason for stopping by today?"

He smiled, showing the deep dimple in his left cheek. "Well, you've got me figured out pretty good. Yeah, there is a reason for my being here today." He gazed at the stream of people exiting the building. "But I don't feel like talking around all these people. Candace's Creamery is around the corner. Did you want to go for some ice cream, or would you rather go for an early dinner someplace?"

She clutched her flowers as she gazed at the late afternoon sky. "We could go to the creamery. Since it's just around the corner we can walk."

He chuckled. "Sounds good to me, dear." They walked to the creamery, hand in hand. Birds twittered from the palm trees, and a slight breeze ruffled through the leaves. Winston squeezed her hand, and she squeezed his back.

They entered the bright, airy creamery moments later. Scents of cinnamon, vanilla and chocolate mingled in the air-conditioned shop. Soft jazz music played, and small groups of patrons dotted the tables, eating ice cream, drinking coffee, working on laptops, reading books and having conversations.

"What'll you have?" He removed his wallet.

She toyed with the petals on the flowers. "I'll have one of those coffee chocolate shakes. Could you get me one of those sandwiches and a pastry, too? I think I am kind of hungry now."

"You got it." He squeezed her shoulder and went to the counter to place his order. He returned to the table minutes later. "He said he'd bring the order when they're done making the shakes."

She nodded. The creamery recently added a cappuccino machine. The sound of the coffee machine filled the air with the grinding clink. He took her hand and massaged her knuckles. "You know, we've come a long way over the past six months."

"I know. I'm so glad we were able to work through our problems." She sighed with contentment. "It feels good to talk to you and have a normal relationship without all of the questions and wondering."

"I know. I just wanted to let you know that I'm sorry for the way I treated you earlier this year. When we got back from the cruise, and I saw my uncle like that—"

She squeezed his hand and placed her fingers over his full lips. "You don't have to explain. I understand you were scared." She sighed as she gazed at the patrons of the ice-cream shop. "I guess in a way I was scared, too. I've also learned a lot about my shortcomings during this relationship."

"You, with shortcomings?"

The server returned to their table with their orders. The delicious scents of chocolate and mocha filled the air as he served their drinks, pastries and sandwiches. "Would you like anything else?" Winston shook his head, waving him away.

After saying a brief prayer she continued their conversation. "Yeah, I have shortcomings, too. You know God didn't make any of us perfect. As both Rachel and Sarah have pointed out to me, I needed to stop being so judgmental toward other people. It's still something I'm praying about. It's hard for me to forgive others, and to believe the best of people."

He stirred his shake before he took a drink. "You mean people like Jordan?"

She sighed. "Yeah, people like Jordan. I've noticed that he hasn't been to my church in awhile, but I was glad that he finally stopped approaching me. I think he's learned to accept the fact that I'm happily involved with someone else."

"You know how the Lord works. Maybe Jordan was going to your church for a reason."

"You mean the sermons might have had an impact on his life? Do you think Jordan might be willing to take the big step and accept Christ as his Lord and Savior?"

"I don't know. The only ones who know about that are Jordan and Jesus, but I do think it's a good sign that he did attend services regularly at one point, don't you?"

She sipped her shake and nodded. "I do think it's a good sign. I know now that I shouldn't have treated him so coldly when he started coming to church. Although it appeared he was coming for the wrong reasons, it now looks like he might have a different agenda on his mind, God's agenda."

"Amen to that." He paused and released her hand. "Did you talk to Amber yesterday?"

She nodded. "Yes, I called her. My long-distance bill has been atrocious since she went back to the farm to live with Mark. But you know, I could see God working in my life then, too."

"Really?" He encouraged her to continue.

"Well, when Mark was going through that stuff with his wife, and I took Amber in, we developed a bonding relationship. I'm now closer to my niece than I ever was in the past, and I think she needs me more now, especially since her parents are no longer together, and she only sees her mother once in a while. Maybe God was setting both of us up for this relationship that we would need in the future."

"Yeah, I can understand why you'd feel that way. It's amazing how things work out sometimes." He paused and finished his sandwich. "So are you ready for this weekend?"

"Yep, I certainly am!"

Over the past six months, Rainy and Winston had taken their youth financial planning seminars to several churches. The seminars became so popular that they could no longer accept all the offers to speak at the churches. Also, since the seminars lasted for several weeks, it was hard to accommodate the wishes of all the churches. "I think we're onto something here," Winston said one Saturday after they'd spoken at another church. "Do you think we need to start doing this and charging people?"

Rainy scoffed. "Winston, do you really think that people are going to pay to attend a youth financial seminar?"

"No, I'm not talking about the youth, I'm talking about the adults. We could always streamline our criteria to fit adults and make it more compact—into, like, a seminar for a day or so and see how that works. A lot of people in the surrounding churches already know who we are. Maybe this is a calling for us in a way. You know God wants us to have control over our finances."

So they started doing financial seminars for adults. Soon they had a small side business going. They weren't making a lot of money yet, but Rainy could see the potential in Winston's idea. "Soon enough, we'll be making enough money on the side to quit our day jobs," he commented happily.

She wasn't sure she agreed with that, but she was enjoying working with Winston, and she could easily see them owning their own business some day, doing financial seminars for African-Americans all over the nation. Just daydreaming about it gave her thrilling goose bumps. It made her feel warm, fuzzy and happy to share a common goal with Winston, and to share their expertise with others.

"Your friend, Rachel, found our advice to be helpful. She's still got a long way to go to finding financial security, but at least she's on the right track."

Rainy nodded. "Yeah, after her car was repossessed, I think that was a good wake-up call for her. She's better with her finances now, not perfect, but better than she used to be." She chuckled softly.

"What's so funny?"

"I was just thinking that when we go out for our weekly lunch, Rachel always has the money to pay for her portion. She hasn't asked me or Sarah to cover for her in ages."

"Ah, I see. Speaking of Sarah, is she still dating that blind man?"

"Oh, you mean Carl? You need to call him Carl instead of 'that blind man.' Sarah gets offended when people call him that. They're still dating, but Sarah has been so hush-hush about this relationship. Usually, she doesn't mind talking about the people she dates and her escapades of dating, but this time she's keeping quiet."

"Uh, oh. Could turn out that he's the right one for her."

"Hmm. Maybe. Sarah hasn't been too optimistic about the dating game. So it's hard to tell if she's serious about this guy or not, or if he's serious about her."

"Well, they've been dating for over six months now, and I think that should account for something, don't you?"

"Yeah, I guess you're right. We'll just have to wait and see what happens between them."

They finished the rest of their meal in silence. The coffee machine continued to putter in the background and the soft jazz music continued to play from the jukebox while patrons spoke in hushed tones. Rainy and Winston were silent as they enjoyed the easy camaraderie of being together. Finally, Winston broke their silent moment.

"Well, there was something I wanted to talk to you about. I never got around to telling you why I came to your job today."

She raised her eyebrows. "Oh? That's right, you haven't."

"Well, first off, this is a celebration. It was six months ago today when I took a plane to your dairy farm in Maryland and asked you to give our relationship a chance and you agreed. Remember?"

Rainy's eyes widened with surprise. They had been a couple for six blissful months, and she still ached to be married to the man. Whenever he held her and kissed her, sparks of happiness flowed through her body like warm butter. So far, she had been hoping and praying that they could take that big step toward marriage.

Although she trusted him, and he said he'd given his doubts over to the Lord, she wondered if he had doubts about having a future with her. Being with Winston filled her with so much euphoria that she desperately wanted to see him everyday in a state of marital bliss.

His deep voice pulled her back to the present time in the creamery. "What are you thinking about?"

She swallowed and toyed with her flowers. "Oh, lots of things," she said with a soft sigh.

Her heart pounded as he caressed her cheek. "Something's bothering you. What is it? Do you miss Amber?

Maybe you should plan another weekend trip to the dairy farm. I could come with you."

She sighed. Winston could be so sweet. "No, it's not that, not right at this moment anyway."

Warm pleasure flowed through her as he stroked the underside of her wrist. "I love you."

"I know. I love you, too." She loved him so much that it hurt not to see him everyday. She ached to hold his hand and to kiss his lips each morning when she went to work and each night when she went to bed. A few other people in her women's Bible study had recently gotten engaged and she'd felt happy for them, but she still wished that she could join the ranks of married couples.

She gazed at the wooden table. Her leftover shake was melting, and rings of beaded sweat covered the plastic cup. The server approached asking if they wanted refills. Winston waved him away.

She suddenly felt a velvety softness pressed into her palm. She gasped when she saw the small box. "Winston?" she breathed. At first she'd figured it was a pair of diamond earrings to match the tennis bracelet he'd purchased for her last birthday. Sarah had this whole thing figured out. She'd predicted after the tennis bracelet that it'd only be a matter of time before Winston proposed to her. Sarah claimed she knew men inside out, and after all the reading she'd done about men and relationships, Rainy felt inclined to believe her, that is, until she predicted her marriage to Winston. Somehow, she didn't think he'd be asking her so soon.

Tears sparkled in her eyes as she quickly glanced around the creamery and noticed the patrons were not paying them any attention as they enjoyed their ice cream.

"I wanted to surprise you, and I see that I've done that." He paused. "I figured if I'd waited and done something special, like having a fancy dinner in a nice restaurant, or asked you on your birthday, it wouldn't have been a surprise. You'd have figured out what I was planning in advance. This way, you didn't even suspect that I was asking you to marry me today. I hope this creamery always stays in business because it's going to be an important place in my life from now on—that is, depending on your response to my question." He paused again and squeezed her hand. "Lorraine Jackson, will you do me the honor of becoming my wife?" he asked softly. "I've been in love with you for a long time, and now I've found the courage to do something about it."

She slowly nodded. "Yes, Winston, I'd be happy to become your wife." They stood and he hugged her. As they shared a long kiss, some of the patrons applauded.

When she got home that evening, and Winston had left, she called her parents first to announce the news. "It's about time he asked you. He already asked our permission a month ago," chimed her mother.

"Huh?" Rainy clutched the phone as she listened to her mother.

"Yeah, baby. He came here uninvited one weekend and said he needed to speak to me and your father."

Rainy twisted the phone cord as she listened to her mother. She smiled as she recalled the events from a few weekends ago. "He said he had some business to attend to that weekend, and he wouldn't tell me what it was," whispered Rainy. Winston was a man of honor and integrity, and she was touched that he asked her parents for her hand in marriage.

After she spoke with her mother, she recalled that she had not gotten the mail that day. She felt like she was floating on a cloud as she walked to her mailbox. She was getting married! She still couldn't believe it. The ring felt like a gifted treasure adorning the third finger of her left hand.

She opened her mailbox and removed the stack of mail. She flipped through the envelopes and stopped as soon as she saw the familiar masculine script adorning the envelope. Just seeing Jordan's broad strokes felt like a mockery on her engagement day. She was tempted to rip the envelope apart and throw it away. "I can't let Jordan ruin my engagement."

Suddenly, she stopped and closed her eyes. She stood beside her mailbox, clutching the letter. A breeze blew, whipping her hair in the wind. *Read the letter,* she sensed a voice telling her.

She gazed at the ring adorning her finger. Her pain and anger toward Jordan now seemed childish and trivial. Her step faltered as she walked to her porch. Birds chirped from the trees as she chose her favorite oak rocker and sat. The floorboards creaked slightly as she rocked in her chair. She said another brief prayer before she ripped the envelope open.

Smoothing the white wrinkled paper, she read the following:

Dear Rainy,

I'm hoping you're giving me the honor of reading this letter. It'll be a miracle if you've read it so far. Rainy, all I can say is that I've been feeling consumed with guilt over the past year since our breakup. I know I've been coming to your church, hoping to win you back. However, after I discovered your happiness with Winston, I knew it was time for me to back away and let you have your peace without me in your life.

Even though things ended badly between us, I have to say that I'd always admired the fact that you always stuck up for your beliefs. I could always get you to change your mind about some things, but when it came to your convictions about God, you held on to your beliefs.

While attending your small church, I've come to understand the meaning of faith. I still have some things that I have questions about, and I haven't accepted Christ yet, but I'm working on getting answers to my questions. I've decided to start attending another church as I work through the issues in my life. Perhaps in due time, I will give the Lord a chance, and I'll accept Him as my Savior.

I hope both you and Winston have a wonderful life together. I feel that you'll probably be engaged and married soon enough, and I just want to wish happiness to both of you.

Again, accept my apologies.

Yours truly,

Jordan Summers

She read the letter a few times, stunned at Jordan's words. She knew in her heart that she'd finally forgiven Jordan for his sins, and she no longer held any bitterness and anger toward his infidelity. She clutched the letter to her chest and said a brief prayer for Jordan's salvation. She gazed at the sun-streaked blue sky before walking back into the house. The screen door banged as she shut it.

She walked into her bedroom and removed her jewelry box. She opened it and found Jordan's engagement ring nestled in the corner. She removed the ring and stroked the perfect diamond. It just didn't feel right to wear Winston's ring while still in possession of Jordan's. She found a padded envelope in her desk drawer. She opened it and dropped the ring inside. She then removed her cream-colored stationery and her pen and wrote her response to Jordan. She told of her forgiveness, and her reasons for returning his ring. After she signed her name, she read the letter several times, hoping the meaning sounded sincere.

She noticed from Jordan's return address that he moved to another county in Florida. She hoped his move helped to provide him with the peace and tranquility he needed to find Jesus. When she was finished addressing the envelope, she dropped it into her purse. She would make a quick stop to the post office the following day to send her small package and letter via registered mail.

Epilogue

The following six months passed in a whirlwind of activity. Rainy was so full of wedding plans that she thought she would burst with excitement.

The day of her wedding dawned bright and clear. "Thank you, Lord, for this beautiful day," she said softly as she opened her window and enjoyed the humid summer air. The palm trees rustled in the breeze, and the air was heavy with the expectation of her wedding day.

A sudden knock sounded on her door. "Rainy, are you awake yet?" Her mother breezed into her home with Amber on her arm. Sarah and Rachel stirred in the living room, opening their eyes to the new day. They had spent the previous night at Rainy's house. They'd spoken of the joys of getting married, and Sarah and Rachel had toasted Rainy, reminiscing about the great times they'd had since she'd arrived in Florida those many years ago.

"I've brought the fixings for your favorite breakfast," her mother stated. Rainy remained silent as she followed her mother into the kitchen. As she broke eggs into a bowl, she told of the smoothness of the wedding plans that day. "Your makeup person should be here shortly and we'll make sure you get to that church on time." Constance opened a package of bacon, peeled the thin slices apart and placed them into a hot skillet.

Hours later, Rainy stood at the entrance to the sanctuary of the church, gazing at the audience. She spotted Cindy, sitting near the front of the church. She was glad Mark and his wife were now attending marriage counseling and that Cindy was now living back at the farm. She noticed Sarah's date, Carl, sitting in a pew near the middle of the church. Sarah seemed happy with Carl and Rainy sensed it was just a matter of time before they got engaged.

She watched Amber walk down the aisle as her flower girl. Her groomsmen, Mark and Winston's brother Deion, escorted both Rachel and Sarah down the aisle. Their dresses were silky midnight blue, and she'd never seen her best friends looking so pretty.

She had been hard-pressed to pick a maid of honor. She had met Sarah and Rachel at practically the same time, and after much thought, prayer and deliberation, she'd decided to make both of them her maids of honor. She knew it was nontraditional, but this was her wedding and that was the way she wanted it to be.

Winston's parents smiled with pride as they watched their son, tears glistening in their dark eyes.

Finally, she took a deep breath as she walked down the aisle on her father's arm. Her flowing white dress was made with lace, seeded pearls and fine silk. She'd never felt more beautiful, and she was pleased to see Winston's startled reaction when he saw her. She felt honored and blessed as they said their vows. She knew deep in her heart that this marriage would flourish since both of them honored the Lord, and she sensed that God was smiling down on them.

* * * * *

Grabill Missionary Church Library
P.O. Box 279
13637 State Street
Grabill, IN 46741

Dear Reader,

I certainly hope you enjoyed Rainy and Winston's story!
I would like to stress the importance of keeping our
Heavenly Father in our lives. No matter what battles
you may be struggling with, you can always lean on
Him, and He will see you through the tough times!

I enjoy hearing from readers. Feel free to visit my
Web site, www.ceceliadowdy.com or e-mail me at
dowdywriter@aol.com. You can also write to me at
the following address:
Cecelia Dowdy
P.O. Box 951
Greenbelt, MD 20768-0951

Blessings,

Cecelia Dowdy

Love Inspired®

LOVING PROMISES

BY

GAIL GAYMER MARTIN

Cynical businessman Dale Levin had a unique
attitude toward marriage—it could never come
close to what his parents shared, and caring for them
showed him that even true love could end. He vowed
never to marry, but when he met widowed Bev Miller
and her boisterous children, he wondered if God was
granting him the happy ending he secretly craved....

Don't miss LOVING PROMISES
On sale March 2005

Available at your favorite retail outlet

www.SteepleHill.com   LILPGGM

Take 2 inspirational love stories FREE!

PLUS get a FREE surprise gift!

Mail to Steeple Hill Reader Service™

In U.S.
3010 Walden Ave.
P.O. Box 1867
Buffalo, NY 14240-1867

In Canada
P.O. Box 609
Fort Erie, Ontario
L2A 5X3

YES! Please send me 2 free Love Inspired® novels and my free surprise gift. After receiving them, if I don't wish to receive anymore, I can return the shipping statement marked cancel. If I don't cancel, I will receive 4 brand-new novels every month, before they're available in stores! Bill me at the low price of $4.24 each in the U.S. and $4.74 each in Canada, plus 25¢ shipping and handling and applicable sales tax, if any*. That's the complete price and a savings of over 10% off the cover prices—quite a bargain! I understand that accepting the books and gift places me under no obligation ever to buy any books. I can always return a shipment and cancel at any time. Even if I never buy another book from Steeple Hill, the 2 free books and the surprise gift are mine to keep forever.

113 IDN DZ9M
313 IDN DZ9N

Name	(PLEASE PRINT)	
Address	Apt. No.	
City	State/Prov.	Zip/Postal Code

Not valid to current Love Inspired® subscribers.

Want to try two free books from another series?
Call 1-800-873-8635 or visit www.morefreebooks.com.

* Terms and prices are subject to change without notice. Sales tax applicable in New York. Canadian residents will be charged applicable provincial taxes and GST. All orders subject to approval. Offer limited to one per household.

® are registered trademarks owned and used by the trademark owner and or its licensee.

INTLI04R   ©2004 Steeple Hill

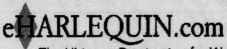

eHARLEQUIN.com
The Ultimate Destination for Women's Fiction

Becoming an eHarlequin.com member is easy, fun and **FREE!** Join today to enjoy great benefits:

- **Super savings** on all our books, including members-only discounts and offers!

- Enjoy **exclusive online reads**—FREE!

- Info, tips and **expert advice** on writing your own romance novel.

- FREE romance **newsletters,** customized by you!

- Find out the latest on your **favorite authors.**

- Enter to win exciting **contests and promotions!**

- Chat with other members in our **community message boards!**

To become a member,
visit www.eHarlequin.com today!

INTMEMB04

Love Inspired®

THE
SISTERS & BRIDES
SERIES BEGINS WITH...

THE BEST
GIFT

BY

IRENE
HANNON

Inheriting her aunt's bookstore—and its handsome manager, Blake Williams—wasn't something A. J. Williams had expected. Like oil and water, the sassy redhead and her conservative co-worker didn't mix. But when forced to work together to solve a problem that affected them both, would their budding friendship lead to the love of a lifetime?

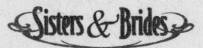

United by family, blessed by love.

Don't miss THE BEST GIFT
On sale March 2005

Available at your favorite retail outlet

www.SteepleHill.com   LITBGIH